9 Tomatoes a Day

Charles S. Darwin III

Anderson, Berkly and Stone Publishers

Published and printed in the United States of America

9 TOMATOES A DAY

See www.9Tomatoesaday.com or www.abspublishers.com to schedule special lectures, obtain special pricing for groups, or to learn more about building farming cooperatives to help eliminate poverty in your area.

9 Tomatoes a Day/ Charles S. Darwin III – 1st ed.

ISBN-13: 978-0615586601

DEDICATION

To the 200,000 lives that were lost in the 2010 Haitian Earthquake. Some may think the loss was senseless. I offer another perspective that those lost lives awakened a host of others that were asleep, giving them a new purpose for walking the Earth. A chance for others to mitigate our fathers wrongs.

To those who work and volunteer to find creative pathways for rebuilding failed nations and to those who inspire new hope and ideas that will eliminate poverty not only in Haiti but also throughout the world.

To those that perpetuate moderation by slaying sacred cows, which otherwise blind reason.

To those who dare nudge the sleeping giant who is beginning to stir, when it fully awakens pessimists will fall away, and humanities highest potential will begin to bloom.

PREFACE

After the 2010 earthquake in Haiti, I began to research the seeds of poverty to learn about the root causes. Poverty is devastating for those living in it; but the impacts of poverty also devastate the environment and economies the rest of us depend on. It is a senseless state of existence caused solely by the short-sided views of a few and the apathy of many. Over three billion people live in poverty, many without any type of sanitation or means of earning a living. If a pandemic ever breaks out, it will surely be due to the misuse of pharmaceuticals and human body waste found in open puddles. Thousands of children die every day due to hunger and exposure to unsanitary living conditions. Many children fall asleep in the dirt hoping they do not wake up, only to endure another torturous day of hunger and flies. There is an answer to this problem and there is a plan; not one based on altruism, but one deeply rooted in good economics and sound environmental policy. It is in our self-interest to turn the poor into producers and consumers, while helping them maintain a robust and traditional culture within their community. 9 Tomatoes a Day lays out a proposal within a fictional setting that seems so real it is hard to believe it could not happen. The book becomes a map on how we can all work together to accomplish what would otherwise seem impossible. 9 Tomatoes a Day can be a snapshot into the future demonstrating, like Ralph Waldo Emerson once proclaimed, "The ancestor of every action is a thought." Decide what kind of world you want to live in, believe you can change what is wrong, and then pick up a shovel.

Charles S. Darwin III

TABLE OF CONTENT

$\mathscr{D}$ARE to fly high above a sea of common thought

to gain astonishing perspectives

vastly different from the cocoons

woven to comfort your blissful slumber.

$\mathscr{D}$ARE to see visions

that fill the sails of mystical ships

carrying the hopes of life deep into distant theaters of play.

$\mathscr{D}$ARE to climb high above the silken threads of comfort.

Enter the turbulent eddies of change and progress.

Sail with purpose away from the ordinary.

Sing your extraordinary song.

Keep your sails full.

INTRODUCTION

David Letterman, the host of *Late Night* asked his guest, President Bill Clinton, a profound question during an interview, "Why do you think, after thousands of years of trying to get things right, humanity is still such a mess?" The thoughtful statesman nodded his head up and down smiling just a little, it was a good question; one he had asked himself all his life as he rose to the World's most powerful position. *"Well David, I guess it is because we have not established a goal: we have not found a common purpose for our existence."*

The first step in achieving a goal is to establish a well-defined purpose. Achieving goals requires a type of sacrifice: sometimes, unimaginable surrender of one's self; sometimes, an entire group must sacrifice something. That is why well-defined statements of purpose are so necessary. Otherwise halfway through an effort many start asking why a sacrifice is required. That is when otherwise great efforts breakdown, groups fall apart, and vultures fly-in to pick through the leftover bones of failure.

For a group to adopt a purpose, a magnanimous leader is required to ignite the first spark. Sometimes a spark ignites simply because what a person is doing looks fun; or perhaps, outside observers see a deeper purpose in the excitement that will eventually benefit everyone. No matter the reason, if one looks hard enough, the method of a movement's genesis reveals itself.

In February 2010, a few weeks after the Haitian earthquake that killed over 200,000 people, Derek Sivers gave a talk at a TED conference titled *"How to Start a Movement."* There are hundreds of such profound lectures available for viewing at www.TED.com: these are "ideas worth spreading."

He shows a video of a bold young man jumping and swinging his arms around like a lunatic, in a hilly park full of people. He was shirtless wearing only a pair of shorts. To some, he looked like a nut. Then to others, what he was doing looked fun. Some may have thought it looked like a great way to exercise, while basking in the Sun. Most everything that generates interest engages a conscious or unconscious need or interest. Within a few seconds, another person joined the impromptu dance mimicking the moves nearly the same way. A follower arrived. The lone nut acknowledged the other person by grabbing his hands while continuing to jump and dance around together on the hillside. Derek proclaims, "This is when the lone nut becomes a leader."

Then something happened, another follower joined the duet. Derek explains further, "Now it's not one lone nut or two lone nuts, there are three people, and three is a crowd and a crowd is news." This movement now has momentum. At that moment, Derek emphasizes, "Movements must be public so they can grow!"

Finally, Derek reveals an unexpected observation, as more and more people join in, they do not follow the leader, he has become a blur; they are following the followers: in movements, the leader fades away becoming just one of the many jumping and dancing within the movement. Some would say the leader was the metaphorical spark that spread into a roaring flame.

Now days, in international political or business networks, practicing altruism, can leave a benevolent leader vulnerable to a pack of marauding wolves. Those who only seek profit have labeled putting the interest of others before self, a sign of weakness. To a predator, it is like a chink in armor oozing blood they can smell miles away. For civilization to change, for the economy and the environment to divert from its current disastrous path towards disorder, a page from the evolutionary playbook of nature demands prominence in the minds of our would-be leaders. Civilization must begin to focus on a com-

mon goal, then begin to practice cooperation and accommo-
dation as religiously as they practice a faith; then be tenacious
in all their efforts.

America, as a group, must wake-up and rip the fickle
foam finger from their hand and realize, as a result of their apathy and lack of intellectual rigor, they are no longer number
one. The American Dream, at present, is only a memory of
great ideas born of principle and vision, intended to serve every individual equally. These ideas are now wandering in a desert trying to find their way back home. And like always they
will, when the next generation takes ownership and learns
from the sins of their fathers, and then changes how business
is conducted around the world and at home. The demagogu-
ery of self-importance and piousness must stop, which will
clear the airways for the wisdom and methods that once made
America strong, and will do so again—cooperation, cooperation, cooperation.

Throughout history, stories filled with bold leaders, cap-
tivated audiences: our species learned from these stories of
heroes, and at times, some lived their lives vicariously through
the hero's adventures. In the beginning, these stories came
alive while groups of people huddled around open fires.

No written words existed in the beginning of the dawn
of civilization. Stories flourished through pictures drawn on
smooth rock surfaces, or passed verbally by elders, from one
generation to the next. These stories contained heroes who
were great hunters or dragon slayers. Thunderbolts, leaping,
like magic from the fingertips of a wizard's hand were adjudicated good or bad, depending on whether it helped others, or
whether it only served to provide more riches for the wizard.

As tribes and their superstitions began to blend, their
power as a group grew and the level of safety afforded them
against other marauding tribes increased. Soon after, societies
began to grow in complexity; as did their stories. Additionally,
due to the blending and the sharing of traditions through story-

telling, trade between people and other tribes began to form various complex types of economies.

As the beginnings of a primal monopoly game began to form, a few big winners emerged who dominated the board. It was not long before the winners began to enslave or tax anyone unfortunate enough to pass over their squares. If players were unable to pay the tax, they suffered punishment, or lost a turn. A great divide began to evolve that separated winners from the losers. The most disturbing outcome of this new game, which few could foretell, was that in the end there could only be one winner.

At first, individual traders gained wealth simply by being more innovative than the others were. These primal entrepreneurs simply created or found something that someone else wanted so bad, they were willing to give up some other prized possession that another person might want. Soon, some learned to increase their wealth and work less by taking with force that which did not belong to them.

Those not able to hold onto their squares containing farms, game, and water, all the things the new societies began to value and hold in high esteem, were doomed to move away to find new lands, or start over.

Class systems began to form into the haves and the haves not: the rich and the poor. Revolts would begin and war would spread across the land. It may have seemed so, but in reality, during these times there were no winners. Some would even say that as individuals began to crave dominion over others, the pathways common to all humanity were lost: this may have been the earliest beginnings of a downward spiral that could destroy an entire species, if left uncorrected.

Because of this new game, as an individual's wealth grew, so did their power to indenture and enslave. Then stories began to contain heroes who became liberators. In some form, a David figure began to dominate the stories of numerous cultures, always standing up and defeating Goliaths. Men like Moses went up to a sacred mountain and came down with universal laws for humankind chiseled into stone tablets: 'thou shall not steal,' was only one of ten new Commandments. 'Thou shall not covet another man's wife' was surely included because of his wife's infidelity, while he was up on the mountain chipping away at rocks, instead of taking care of her back home. These new laws, regardless of origin or intent, provided the foundational rules for communal living that created order, stability, and safety. While making it easier for men to go "rock chipping," instead of staying at home.

As the economic divide widened, the occurrence of wars became more prevalent. To the victors also came the right to create and enforce laws that benefited mostly them. In order to survive, Kings and Warlords entered into treaties; compromises allowed for the sharing of power and making decisions. A few treaties allowed the less fortunate to participate in decisions that involved their communities. This began the origins of governments: a great and benevolent concept with a noble purpose, but one that usually shielded the greedy from their evil wrongdoing. Many of these wrong doers began to use the power of government to increase their wealth, instead of using the thugs of old. Much like the United States Congress and Senate does today; legislators make laws that put people in jail for the same crimes they perpetrate, but have given themselves immunity for committing. Practices like that are not only considered unjust to those imprisoned, but truly obscene and worthy of rebellion. The evil and greed of these types of hideous scoundrels became ever more difficult to detect, as the government grew larger, with more decision makers to blame.

Today, our stories need heroes who step away from the propaganda and orchestrated confusion found in modern day media and politics, to call evil evil and greed greed no matter the reason, be it national security or corporate profit. Our present need is for heroes who face danger not for a cause, a state, a vote, or a flag but for the sake of humankind. Most notably, putting their individual lives on the line for the betterment of millions.

This story brings to light many unique types of heroes: First, the human kind; next a detailed Program for Change, still another a reality show, and finally the Accomplishment. Yes, you may soon be persuaded that an accomplishment can also be a hero. The most improbable hero, however, is a technology that uses waste to power industry and allows joy and wellbeing to bloom in a community. The primary thesis of the story, however, is that any part is only a small portion of the whole. One man, using leverage, can move a boulder; but a community focused on a common goal under one flag of purpose, can level mountains that block pathways to higher achievement; and finally, the measure of success is universal happiness, not gold.

Initially this story's protagonist looks like an individual hero: a lone nut. Soon, however, as a common core of experience evolves and individual perspectives swirl into a larger vision, followers begin to follow followers, and the focus on the protagonist's achievements blurs as he evolves into a coach merely helping to keep the vision on track. The group effort begins to take over, morphing into a larger more inclusive hero, the Program for Change, ultimately resulting in the Accomplishment. The combined efforts of the group prove that in all matters, tenacity defies defeat. The Accomplishment demonstrates that ordinary people who do minor heroic deeds can counterpoint bad government policy and bring back righteousness to an empire that has lost its way.

In effect, the "Program for Change," becomes a hero as it erects a fort and outlines a clear pathway leading to its gate. This metaphorical fort keeps detractors away from the Accomplishment located within. The Program helps ordinary people, living in poverty and squalor, to work themselves out of those conditions. It provides a structure for maintaining order and management. It is a financial model providing education, food, and healthcare, ownership of homes and businesses, and yields cash flows. It is a business plan for would-be heroes to follow and help implement.

Some might view the Program as an altruistic hero, but that perception is incorrect. This hero is all about good business and effective government. There is nothing altruistic about it. The Program is working shamelessly in its own self-interest to keep the game alive by following the laws of nature not man.

The Program is trying to reignite the global economy, defuse the population bomb, reduce greenhouse gas emissions, and eliminate the breeding grounds of terrorism.

In doing so, however, the Program raises the unwanted attention of those who fear they will lose control, power, and profit. Winning that challenge becomes a violent risky effort, indeed. It becomes an unsung effort that only a handful of trusted visionaries know about. Then, before the mendacious powerful realized what happened, they are forced into a compromise that brought about a profitable peace for all to enjoy. They had no choice; a wolf used their own deceitful tactics against them.

A Reality Show, produced by an insightful company, becomes a hero that rallies millions of people using entertainment; it reveals to them a common and fulfilling purpose for living. The Reality Show is the conduit through which other groups of potential heroes learn about the Program. The actions that result are sustainable and lasting. Millions of deep and lasting footprints left behind for others to follow. Without the efforts of this hero, the Program would never have gained the momentum needed to succeed.

The biggest hero in this story, however, is the Accomplishment. It lives in the fort created by the Program for Change; it must remain protected. It has become an international superhero among lesser heroes. Proof that humanity can work outside individual self-interest. It demonstrates that making decisions that benefit the least among us will benefit us all. It blazes trails into new territories for the Program and for more heroes to follow.

The Accomplishment would not have happened, however, unless all the different types of heroes had showed up; even the most improbable hero, a machine that prevents sickness and offers solutions to complex environmental problems; a machine that is central to the environmental and conservation goals that the Program for Change seeks to pursue and enforce.

This story starts with an impetuous, soldier in the United States Air Force who traveled the world living in different cultures, and later became an industrialist after his enlistment. Years later, with his own company in financial crisis, he began to study multiple problems and to develop ways to solve them using one elegant solution. Solutions emerged for problems that plagued both his life and the lives of millions of others: both the rich and the poor would benefit. Capitalism and socialism merged by a common goal created the economic diversity that was lacking in the past. As a result, commerce began to expand and jobs flourished.

The reluctant warrior turned industrialist developed a plan that offered a solution that could help billions of people by merely lighting a metaphorical match. From the light given off by a small flickering flame, he would watch as hundreds of millions of ordinary people experienced an epiphany that caused them to want to help fan the spreading fires of success. Collectively, these new heroes accomplished a result that promised a brighter tomorrow for all of humanity, but especially for those who were the most deprived.

This story details a Program for Change that eliminates poverty simply by building farming cooperatives. Each participating family receives ownership of a home and a portion of the business. The costs for these are equivalent to harvesting just 9 Tomatoes a Day. As a result, global markets expand overnight in a way that pulls the entire worldwide economy out from a slump that resulted from a lack of vision and leader-ship.

Some wicked wizards accused of being consumed with greed, are ultimately revealed to be heroes who had simply lost their way and could not, until now, find their way back to a pathway common to us all.

This victory happens because millions of Americans and people from other nations watch a game show and partic-ipate in the outcome. The viewers and their lives light up as they help Haitians rebuild their nation, simply by supporting celebrities who pool their talent, and make the impossible happen.

Building supply and equipment manufacturers began to advertise and help with the farm construction, realizing that new markets would open up for their products. Amazing new technologies emerge for growing food and turning crops into carbon sequestering manufactured goods. Worldwide, the lives of viewers and those receiving support begin to have more meaning and purpose.

Mostly, the viewers' lives improve because of the new jobs created in their own communities that result from supply-ing the needs and wants of the newest consumers entering the global markets. From this point on, the word globalization will invoke ideas of opportunity, and economists will need to rethink their theories.

The victory, however, requires the defeat of detractors who are terrified that they would lose control of their cheap work force and the means to keep them dependent. Further-more, it is feared once people are educated, they are empow-ered; then they become much harder to convince that natural resources belong to corporations and those in power; not the community.

The coach steps up to that challenge unafraid to don Wolves' clothing to hide his Sheppard's persona. Once again, he will begin to use the tactics of predators, to protect the lambs. The hideous realities of human greed he learned long ago, on a mountainside along the remote boarder of Turkey and Iran, and subsequently learned to hide in the depths of his mind, once again return to the forefront of his life so that the seeds of prosperity can take root.

1

Seeds of Poverty

Perspective is everything. Consider Napoleon. To his homeland, he was a hero. To humanity, he was equivalent to Hitler. Few heroes can satisfy their homelands and simultaneously the rest of humanity. That is, unless their actions benefit everyone including the poorest amongst us. And so it was with the early explorers.

The human body, depending on age, is approximately 60% water. The measureable part of the Earth consists of 70.9% water. On Earth, water is the foundation of all sentient life. Without water, Earth's great experiment would look much different. With amazing precision, the path of water on Earth mimics the pathway traveled by civilization. It appears a folly of individuals, groups, and idealisms crashing against rock after rock, on its way back home to the source.

Go to any mountaintop and begin to follow a creek. Eventually, the confluence of other brooks and streams form a raging river that carries all that dare to enter, back home to the sea. The sea is every person's beginning, and everyone's destination. It is a library storing a wealth of knowledge and understanding. The sea is a place where one can drink and feed until sated; before returning to the mountaintop, destined to once again, restart another tortuous journey; perhaps each successive start begins with a clearer purpose, and better-defined goals.

To begin, no person knows what he or she will encounter during their travels. No one really knows what rocks he or she will chip off along the way that increases the burden for those that follow. For those open to new exciting experiences, they find the journey is no longer oriented around self, but instead orients towards relieving the surfeit burdens of others. Many little lives, influenced by seemingly inconsequential events, will always meet up in the end; it is the decisions made where streams bifurcate that make all the difference. This story epitomizes how many little lives and events can culminate in one magnificent goal with a remarkable purpose.

It was in the summer of 1765, in a remote area of what is now Nigeria. A mother and daughter are hiding, under a pile of palm frawns. A few moments before, they were fleeing from slavers who had attacked their village in the middle of the night. The daughter, Adanech, which means, "She has rescued them," whispers to her mother, Abrihet meaning, "She has made it light,"

"Mother I am scared."

Abrihet quietly replies, perhaps knowing these would be her last words, "Be brave, everyone is scared, do not give into your fear, or you will die. Then my gift to the world will be lost. Whatever you do in this moment, do it to survive. If you survive, you will have a chance to make a difference. Survive, that is all I ask of you now. Make your life mean that for which you were named, rescue them from themselves."

Screams replaced the quiet of the night. The mother and daughter discovered. After the terror and unimaginable violence caused by the depraved evil, Abrihet lay mutilated with her life slowing returning to the soil, where the hidden waters will safely carry her soul back home.

Adanech survived. Dragged out of the forest and into the middle of the camp, her captures chained her to the rest of the survivors. From there, she would be loaded onto a boat and taken to a new colony in the West Indies.

Years later, on a stormy night, waves were crashing down onto a ship, coming from all directions. Lightening seemed to jump out of the surrounding water giving only the slightest glimpse of the terror that surrounded the retched boat and its cargo of slaves. A pitiless seaman having years of experience at sea, and having indulged every degeneracy known to humanity, laid on the deck in fear for his immoral life. It would seem, however, that the carrying capacity of evil that any one man can endure is limited. For after the images of his crewmates washing overboard, blended with the foul smells of death rising from the bilge, he could take no more. Holding onto the main mast, the lost soul raised his head to the heavens and screamed, "Is such wickedness worth the graces of God?"

When a person comes to a crossroad in their life, voluntarily or by a force of nature, it is a fifty-fifty chance which way to go. The best question to ask before making any decision is, which way will benefit everyone, even the least among us. The seaman made his choice and the future was established.

The weather was freezing, and the snow rose up to the knees of a little eight-year-old boy. It was Jan 5, 1941 in the Nazi extermination camp, Chelmno, in Poland. The boy Adara, meaning the Noble one, and his mother were standing in line. "Adara, listen to me quickly. The guards are going to take you away. Listen to me Adara; do as they tell you. Do everything you must, to survive. You have to survive Adara, do this so you may tell others what happened. Survive so you can keep this from ever happening again. Adara these men and what they do, they do not represent what the world is or what it can be, you must find a way to change things Adara."

The transition to becoming a man is difficult enough without the added pressures of doing so as a young boy in the mist of hate, prejudice, and ignorance, so absurd, it would break the backs of most grown adults. Nevertheless, transition Adara did, and the terrible lessons of his early life helped to bring together a civilization that had been slowing tearing apart because it had once lost its way.

Some say it all started when Columbus 'discovered' the Americas in 1492. Most say it has always been our nature, that it is indeed primal. It first reared its menacing head before we began to knuckle walk: the need to dominate, to make those who would be our equals subservient. Somehow, somewhere, humankind missed the mark: for some reason, the concept was lost that decisions made that benefit the least amongst us benefit us all.

As the great sailing ships from the northern European expansion began to colonize new lands south of the equator, their officers and men looked upon the sun-darkened natives not as human beings but as members of another species. They had no government; they could not speak English, Belgian, Spanish, French, or Portuguese; by all standards known to civilized man, they were ignorant: so as a result, their lands and resources were claimed for European royalty, not the Europeans. Natives forced into manual labor, without compensation, worked until they died. Hands amputated, women, and children raped all to force the fathers to meet their unreasonable quotas. This, however cruel, was nothing new.

In the early days, governments like gods were simply a reflection of the personalities of those in power, not the people who fell under their influence. The fathers of the people in power were taught that using force and bribery builds even greater wealth--and that could be used to purchase more power! Those ethics continued to fester in the minds of ship captains and explorers and spread while they walked upon new lands witnessing and claiming the bounty of natural resources and untapped labor for their King or Queen.

Royalty, landowners, and warlords did the same thing in their own lands. For thousands of years, those who were weaker and less ambitious suffered unfair taxes, who also took out loans they could never pay back; or were enslaved when all they wanted was to drink the water and work the land now owned and claimed by force, by those deemed by their gods to be superior. Yes, a divine right and God's favor was misused to justify why one person was able to reward or punish at will.

The Royalty formed wholly owned Corporations, in reality monopolies, intended to facilitate trade between the homelands and the newly established colonies. Excess natives, not needed for local farms, were auctioned-off to others as slaves, after enduring thousands of miles of grueling travel at sea, stacked into boats like cargo.

The colonies worked under mandates to grow specific crops and ship them back to the homeland. Back home, value was added to the commodities. The new value added products sold throughout the homeland and then came back to the colonies but at much inflated prices. The homeland forbade the colonies from adding any type of value to their crops, metals, or any other natural resource. These were the seeds of what society now views as poverty.

It is time to stop ignoring and acknowledge those that our fathers channeled into a life of scarcity, and ultimately this attitude change will come about for selfish, profitable reasons. As the world's economies begin to crash, and global environmental challenges begin to mount, humanity has the opportunity and the need to bring into the markets hundreds of millions if not billions of new consumers. As a result, new jobs will appear and free trade will expand. Most importantly, populations will decrease because of access to education and birth control, improved farm practices, and the decreasing cost of food. Green house gases diminish because farm practices begin to specify the use of wastes and renewable crops to manufacture goods and services that sequester carbon. These new commodities will eventually decrease the need for fossil fuels, and generate bold technologies that will ultimately have a positive global impact.

Natural selection blessed humanity with an extraordinary level of complexity that allows us to reason, change, and rapidly adapt to our environments: to build wondrous gadgets that gives humanity more leisure time to perfect their individual art. It is now time to use that reason to alter the course of humanity by coming to the aid of those less fortunate while at the same time helping ourselves. Not doing so will seal the fate of humanity. Doing so will at least insure cooperation amongst all nations as we equally face the new challenges of sea level rise and global climate change.

Two absolutes bind together the very rich and the very poor; the first is we will all die; the second is that there are no pockets in heaven or hell. The only riches that have any eternal meaning are the footprints we leave behind for others to follow.

For America, France, and most of northern Europe including Belgium, an opportunity of great importance exists. There is a chance to correct egregious errors of judgment made during a time of ignorance: it is a chance to correct problems they caused and then ignored over 300 years ago: it is a chance to make enormous environmental improvements and economic profit while doing so.

The French-owned Isle of Hispaniola, now split into the two independent nations Haiti and the Dominican Republic, was unique amongst all the colonies. For years it provided 80% of the coffee, sugar, cocoa, and other commodities sold throughout Europe. This was due to the hard work of slaves that outnumbered their European owners by a ratio of 35 to 1. Violently and unmercifully, the ancestral African villages fell to slavers and pirates who then replanted the villagers in Hispaniola and the Americas. Families and strangers forced to work on the desolate island that had once sustained only a few indigenous Arawak natives, who were also tortured and then enslaved. Finally, one-day things changed.

The only successful slave rebellion in the world started, and the Hispaniola slaves freed themselves from their European owners. Unfortunately, they never freed themselves from those more ambitious and greedy: the evil wizards: Wolves, whose national citizenship has always been irrelevant. The freed slaves were still without ownership of the land, access to education, or the benevolent leadership they needed to take advantage of the bountiful resources they had at their fingertips. Trade restrictions and import taxes kept any farmers in these impoverished areas from adding value to their crops that could make them competitive with European or American commodities. The American President Thomas Jefferson, one of the founders of independence, and liberty and justice for all, refused to acknowledge the new free nation of ex-slaves, for fear that their rebellion would spread to America and perhaps his own farm of slaves.

For the next two hundred and forty years, short-lived dictators and corrupt leadership plagued the new country, and the people became pawns in a game whose only purposes were to make the rich richer and to feed delusions of power and control of a few miserable souls.

One American man's desperation soon mixed with the misery from a confluence of strangers, still separated by oceans, during the world's worst economic collapse. The global economic tragedy followed Haiti's most catastrophic earthquake. All these events began to blend and evolved into a global vision to turn the tide of yesterday's wrongs and to help lift the poorest amongst us from the grip of poverty and indecency.

The economic collapse served to remind everyone where we came from and of the fragile fabric holding any success together. A fabric that if torn apart, can send all of us back to square one without collecting two hundred dollars, having to restart the monopoly game: but this time, armed with nothing but our wits and charms to use while building a new life. Soon, the whole world was watching and helping. Soon, the confluence and stories of many lives would begin to merge into a stream flowing in the same direction.

2

Dark Death, Enlighten Birth!

All things being equal, why is it, one community living in what society calls poverty can be happy, productive, and clean; while another is miserable, dirty, and without dignity?

"GET IN HERE!" Sergeant Stone Richards once again abruptly beckoned into the office of the unit commander, a tall, redheaded, dodgy ROTC trained lieutenant. Stone had just completed a stack of reports filled with problems needing solutions.

Working with this officer was secondary to his real purpose but yet essential to his cover. The lieutenant dressed Stone up and down, repeating his famed speech, "Any asshole can find a problem. Start finding solutions or you will be counting your teeth as they march single file out your whoopie cakes!"

Stone laughed thinking that was the most creative two words the lieutenant ever rubbed together.

"Didn't think you had the vocabulary, Lieutenant, keep it up. I'll be in the office readying my teeth for the parade."

At that moment, however, a light bulb turned on; a moment that typically molds and shapes a person began to unfold. Stone got the message loud and clear, but for a reason altogether different from the one, the lieutenant had intended. For Stone the comment made him aware and highlighted his talent for reacting to and finding solutions for difficult problems. A personal trait he had not focused on before. He resolved at that moment that every problem had a solution; it only took will, patience, and tenacity to see a problem resolved. Stone had always been an optimist.

He deplored pessimists, always proudly declaring they see the problems, no matter how obvious they stood out for others to see; but not once willing to do the work, or risk what it takes to help push the boulder over the top of the mountain. Pessimists, however, are always more than glad to join a hard-won victory party and bask in the glorious light thrown off by those that took the chance.

In Stones position, he saw a mountain of problems that reached all levels every day. His job was to track down the source of those problems; especially the ones that involved the military if they grew tentacles that reached outside its boundaries. Finding the history, involvement, and mysteries behind challenges, then planning creative solutions would be Stones ultimate use of his talent.

From his point of view, he had no other choice; he needed a distraction to fight the demons that plagued his memories. The demons that haunted him were artifacts from past military missions that would otherwise cause him to lose any remaining faith he had in government or mankind. He had seen the "*Dollars of Death*" and uncovered their masters.

Years later, Stone learned it is a matter of perspective. That is, whose shoes you are walking in at the time that de-termines the measure of any mission's success. Nonetheless, his military experience drove him into the service of others helping to countervail the efforts of the greedy that keep the poor hungry and without the necessities to live.

Stone's childhood home was modest. His father worked for a communications company during the day, at night and on weekends, he looked over his flock as a minister. His mother was strong and principled. They were a church going family: every time the doors opened, both god and mother consorted to make sure of that.

Stone loved the community created by the church, its people, and their good intentions; but he fought to understand the religious dogma. He would eat at the "dinners on the ground" but never could swallow their ideology. Religious history revealed volumes on intent. To him religious ideology and blind faith flew in the face of fact, and then stood in the way of advancing civilization, liberty, and innovation. The coffin was nailed shut when he studied that in 1616, during the Roman Catholic Church's Congregation of the Index, a decree was issued suspending *De revolutionibus* until it could be "corrected," on the grounds that the "Earth moves and the Sun does not." That it "...was false and altogether opposed to the Bible scriptures." The same decree outlawed any idea that defended the mobility of the Earth or the immobility of the Sun, or that attempted to reconcile these assertions with biblical scripture. In 1633, Galileo stood convicted of heresy for "following the positions of Copernicus, which ran contrary to the "true sense and authority of Holy Bible." Galileo was under house arrest for the rest of his life. Then look what happened to Jesus when he started speaking like a mystic in contradiction to the teachings of the Jews. That did not end well for him either.

Stone had faith, however, faith that hard work, patience, and inspiration would finally reveal all hidden truths. God instead became a Librarian to Stone: a well that springs forth nature's knowledge and inspiration. The Librarian does not dabble in morality. That results from a lost battle. Morality is an artifact of the victor's ego and bias; thinking they can build a better society simply by forcing others to believe in an embellished doctrine of God's will, written by the victors, "We have an offer you cannot refuse." To achieve that, however, a prophet or idol is required. In one case, a victor became the prophet saying he spoke to God directly, learning every detail how his followers should live, down to how many stones they should use after they defecate. Then he went about killing everyone who said he was crazy. Another group focused on their interpretations of the peaceful teachings of Jesus, as written in the Gospel of Thomas. How anything Jesus murmured from his lips, turned into the Inquisitions of the Catholic Church is beyond human understanding. Except to say, the lust for power and control will climb into any bed with any parasite, to achieve its goal. Lust for power is an aphrodisiac that should never be trusted, in any form. In saying (21) of the Gospel of Thomas, Jesus replies to Mary:

Mary said to Jesus, "Whom are Your disciples like?"

He said, "They are like children who have settled in a field which is not theirs. When the owners of the field come, they will say, 'Let us have back our field.' They (will) undress in their presence in order to let them have back their field and give it back to them. Therefore I say to you, if the owner of a house knows that the thief is coming, he will begin his vigil before he comes and will not let him into his house of his domain to carry away his goods. You, then, be on your guard against the world. Arm yourselves with great strength lest the robbers find a way to come to you, for the difficulty which you expect will (surely) materialize. Let there be among you a man of understanding. When the grain ripened, he came quickly with his sickle in his hand and reaped it. Whoever has ears to hear, let him hear."

At the time, according to the sayings of Jesus in the Gospel of Thomas, there were many disciples of Jesus talking about his teachings: many of them, apparently not getting his message right.

If one reads with the knowledge of evolutionary cosmology, including that the Earth revolves around the Sun, and that everything connects to everything else, there is nothing in the stories, told in the bible that could discredit the wisdom, goodness, or righteousness that poured from every one of Jesus' actions or sayings. But there is plenty in the Bible that twisted the sayings of Jesus for seemingly nefarious purposes. For instance, Jesus never declared he was a prophet or a son of God; but some 60 years later Mathew, Mark, Luke, and John said he was in their writing and the theocrats, seeing opportunity, went along with it. When asked, in the Gospels of Thomas, removed from the bible by Emperor Constantine, in saying (77), Jesus says:

"It is I who am the light which is above them all. It is I who am the All. From Me did the All come forth, and unto Me did the All extend. Split a piece of wood, and I am there. Lift up the stone, and you will find Me there."

In Thomas saying (3), Jesus says,

"...the Kingdom of God is inside of you, and it is outside of you. When you come to know yourselves, then you will become known, and you will realize that it is you who are the sons of the living Father. But if you will not know yourselves, you dwell in poverty, and it is you who are that poverty."

If the "Father" takes on the characteristics of nature or the cosmos, from which everything evolved, and evolutionary theory confirms, Jesus stands out not as a prophet, or a son of God, but an insightful observer of the Universe that wanted to share his insight with others. His sayings parallel Taoism, more than any other ideology at the time. The only sin Jesus died for was the slothfulness of individuals, who could have stood up against ignorance perpetuated by blind-faith, and the arrogance of theocrats; but instead they hid away, afraid to positively affect destiny.

History illustrated, to Stone, that religions of any kind based on the teachings of Jesus is a blasphemy against his true intent based on the 114 sayings of Jesus written down in the Gospels of Thomas. It is obvious why orders to destroy and discredit these sayings of Jesus were attempted; and continue today, there is no profit in them. Jesus says every one is a God, and with that, there would be no need for a religion.

Then there would be no moral control by a theocracy. Stone wondered what would have happened if history reversed itself, and only the Gospel of Thomas was published, and the rest of the current bible had been declared the bantering of narcissists. What kind of a world would we have now if the knowledge of today's science, replaced the ignorance of the past that once required brilliant new theories to remain within the wrongheaded interpretations of misguided scriptures? How much faster would have civilization advanced ethically and technically?

...And He took him and withdrew and told him three things. When Thomas returned to his companions, they asked him, "What did Jesus say to you?"

Thomas said to them, "If I tell you one of the things which he told me, you will pick up stones and throw them at me; a fire will come out of the stones and burn you up."

Gospel of Thomas saying (13)

Preserving stories is the way complexity in a society builds. Storage of memory is how complexity in the entire universe builds. Otherwise, each new generation would have to relearn old lessons: that would not be efficient. Nature's librarian, however, spoke to Stone in various ways other than scriptures. Stone heard stories coming from the trunks of trees when he used a stethoscope, listening for fluids rushing from the roots, on their way up to the top of the branches. These were stories formed from the first principles of life.

His favorite Greek Philosopher Nikos Kazantzakis would talk with almond trees sometimes asking it, "Friend tell me about God." It was then the almond tree would bloom. The Greek almond trees never bloomed for Stone when he visited them, but indeed he though he saw God a few times, while picnicking under the branches with tourist girls.

Stone could also read a billion years worth of history from rock formations that comprised landscapes. He would stand on the edge of the Grand Canyon, or on the summit of Mount Olympus, gazing at the stars reminded how small humanity can be, compared to the grandeurs of the universe. He would be reminded how petty and unimportant humanity remains, but also how important they could become to the survival of life when the level of gases fueling stars begin to change.

It took trillions upon trillions of failed experiments for atoms to evolve into the complex machines humanity now represents. And when the day comes, as the Sun begins to swell into a red giant, or perhaps, just the slightest life giving parameter on Earth falls out of balance, all the energy that it took for atoms to build humanities current level of reality will be lost. The experiment would have to start all over again. That is, if humanity cannot find a way to adapt and survive the test that will ultimately propel them into deep space, in search of a new planet to call home: a new home where another story of genesis can originate. To achieve that goal, means learning to share and live in close quarters within galactic space ships all nations built cooperatively. It will take thousands upon thousands of light years to find a new home, and living in such conditions will take extraordinary teamwork. Something humanity needs to begin practicing immediately here on Earth, because thus far during 10,000 years of recordable history, we still have a long way to go. A good first step is to learn from our history, and then remove the superstitions that infect our children at early ages, and divide cultures that would otherwise work towards a common goal.

For his part, Stone turned away from the churches need to "spread the good word" while imposing their brand of good intentions on civilizations that had been living sustainably otherwise for thousands of years; that is, until they were told by the missionaries the embarrassing news that they were walking around naked. It was oafs like Leopold II, masquerading as a noble King of Belgium, who duped all the other northern nations, during the Berlin Conference, into believing he was taking ownership of the Congo to spread Christianity and help to pacify the region for trade. After cutting off hands, burning villages, and raping all the women and children that could be rounded-up, over 10 million natives died so that glutton could satiate his thirst for wealth. But then, Leopold only used the playbook of the British Empire, who sent missionaries around the world to pacify the aboriginals so the ports would be safe for trade. It is not recorded how many native people were killed by "God's" disciples, but just one dying senselessly was too many. These things were evidence for Stone that the Bible is of man, while the laws of nature were of god. It was unadulterated lunacy imagining a god spending billions of years to build a sand castle, only to maliciously kick it apart. Would anyone follow a leader, or a god, such as that? Nevertheless, he provides a great excuse for the inexcusable; "...it was god's will."

These stories of indiscretion, no matter the intentions followed Stone into his years of manhood. This period was to form the core of Stone's humanity: the core upon which he felt government's duty to its people should be, and made him suspicious of any holy roller's credentials.

Stone enlisted in the Air Force when he was 18 years old. He was brash and impatient for adventure. His testing revealed he was a match for a stealthy branch of the military known as the National Security Agency: a job that also required him to qualify for a top-secret clearance.

After boot camp and technical training, his first assignment was on the Island of Crete at a small air station. It was there he learned hard lessons about good and bad government. Some called it politics. Stone learned to call it overlooked criminal activity—when corrupt government officials, not governments, would use their power to enrich themselves and those that got them to power. For example, the corrupt congressional pirates, that takes stock tips, instead of cash brides, for doing the bidding of their corporate benefactors.

Immediately upon his arrival in Crete, Stone moved off base into a small village next to a protected harbor that opened into the Aegean Sea. Friends "in the know" helped him to find a house to rent. Years later, in retrospect, it seemed the house selection was deliberate. The property owner turned out to be the influential police chief; a man for which a few cartons of American cigarettes, some bottles of Jim Beam, and a bag of money for the bigger transgressions could open a world of forgiveness, if not oversight.

A few months later, Stone, collaborated with some of his diving friends to purchase a forty-foot Greek motor-sailing vessel. That one decision to join in the purchase became a fork in the road that set a new course for his life offering a new destiny.

The Greek village Stone lived in opened his eyes to a world he had never seen. These people were poor, worked hard, and lived sparsely. They had no knowledge of their poverty. They had no televisions to give them a comparison. They were happy, proud, and full of life. Music and dance were as important to them as air. They had everything they needed. The only difference between the Europeans that would vacation on this Mediterranean home of mystical gods, and the natives, were their clothing; and on the beach, where bathing suits were an afterthought, there seemed to be no difference at all. Of course, the Greek villagers wanted more if they could get it, but the wanting of more did not consume them. They dealt with the wanting of more, much like shade under a tree. If they could find it, they would take advantage and use it. If shade did not exist, they would continue living without it.

The old, disabled, and widowed were all taken care of the same, even if they were not blood relatives: they were family, nonetheless. The Greeks loved each other and if not, respected an individual's right to exist and be different. Everyone had a place and a job. The old widows dressed in black, each with thick-combed gray mustaches, would sit on the cobble stone streets all day and whack children with willow sticks who were too noisy or running too fast, screeching universal words Stone could not understand, but instinctively knew their intended purpose. They were the street cops and baby sitters.

Crazy people that scolded trees that would not bear fruit and jabbed fingers in the air, served to remind the others of their blessings. Extra food was cooked and taken to the homes of these people making sure they ate: so they knew they were not alone.

The military paid careful attention to Stone's activities because of the mischief he would get into with his boating and diving friends, as well as the parties he would attend in the village that lasted for days. All activities of military personnel working for the NSA suffered close constant monitoring. It seemed that his friends were in the import and export business finding and transporting antiquities. Apparently, his partners were using their boat for illicit purposes and his Landlord was growing richer for it; unknown to Stone.

One afternoon as Stone was leaving the secure facility, the Base Commander's secretary asked him to come into the office.

"Airman Richards, the Colonel wants to see you in the conference room."

Stone stepped into the secretary's office and entered the conference room via her doorway. He stood in front of a long conference table lined with formal chairs. Maps of the Middle East, North Africa, Central and Eastern Europe, and Russia lined the walls with colorful pins protruding out of every known hot spot. Stone was involved with most of their neighbors to the immediate east and south. On a few occasions, he posed as a college student using friendships with Albanian and Yugoslavian tourist girls, to enter those countries while they were still under Soviet control. Incidentally, only communist party members working for the government traveled, and for some reason they all ended up where Stone and his military friends would party until the wee morning hours. During that time, the game of misinformation was sometimes as tricky as gathering demonstrable field intelligence. When Stone first arrived, at least two Airmen were already missing, presumable drugged by girls and carried out to waiting Soviet trawlers that were constantly monitoring the base that was always monitoring them. As a result, Stone, took the precaution to order unopened bottles of Jim Beam or Metaxa, and never used mixers or a glass when he drank in a bar. He drank straight from the bottle and carried it with him anywhere he went in the bar. If by chance, he left it unattended, he ordered a fresh unopened bottle.

Military personal, especially those with high-level clearances, encountering eastern bloc "tourists" were required to fill-out contact report forms; therefore, the effort had to be worth the trouble. The good part of that deal was if anyone forgot their girlfriend's name, all they had to do was ask the Office of Special Investigations for an update. Because of his drinking precautions, Stone constantly forgot the names of his "girlfriends."

The Colonel was standing in front of a map of the Middle East. One finger was on a pin near the Iranian border, one on Kabul in Afghanistan, and the other on a pin in the center of Lebanon. The year was 1975, just months before the Lebanese Civil War began. The operations unit was monitoring the militarization of the Palestinian refugee population, after the arrival of the PLO guerrilla forces sparked an arms race amongst the different Lebanese political factions. In another region, chatter was building from the Marxist-Leninist government of the Democratic Republic of Afghanistan asking for help from the Soviet President Leonid Brezhnev to fight the Mujahedeen. In Iran, groups of Islamist students and militants, were being monitored, who eventually generated a pivotal episode that caused an incumbent American president to lose an election. These were the years before the Iranian students took over the American Embassy which toppled the Shaw and caused a distraction so huge that the Soviets were allowed to enter Afghanistan unchallenged. In other terms, d1 to a4; check. It was a defining blow to American prestige in the region. Anyone familiar with the theater of play knew there was a stink permeating through that area, getting ready to expand across all borders. There was a deadly game of chess going on, and Crete was central to the entire outcome. Nevertheless, there were nefarious actors who saw opportunity and profit in the confusion and leaped into action.

"Thank you for stopping by."

"Was there really a choice Colonel?"

"No, this is called being polite, sit down and shut-up."

Then two other people in civilian clothing, introduced only as military consultants, accompanied them. They pulled out pictures of statues, vases, and pottery that looked old and chipped. They asked Stone if he ever had seen any of these articles. Stone answered only in the Iraklion museum.

They explained the antiquities came from Greek waters and were on their way to London. His friends were using him. If caught, Stone would see the inside of a Greek prison and the Air Force would be powerless to help. Stone asked them what they wanted him to do. The answer was prepared in a ten-page "eyes only" document that outlined the current situation and what they proposed Stone could accomplish. They wanted Stone to continue with his current relationships but take on a larger roll. He would be given some more field training and resources that would enable him to move up further into the organization and find out who and what that group was all about. He reluctantly agreed, but only after the Colonel took him into his private office to discuss the challenge further.

Stone he started, "You didn't ask for this but here we are. You are in the best situation to find out what we are really dealing with. More than the stealing of antiquities is at stake here. We are finding heroin and other drugs in this exact building where everyone is suppose to have a top-secret clearance. We are also finding counterfeit dollars spreading through Greece, Germany, and Turkey. I think they are connected. If you choose not to take on this assignment all I ask is that you do not talk with anyone about this meeting and continue with your normal routine."

Stone knew what he was being asked to do was illegal and could land him in a foreign jail. The Air Force was officially, not a part of the program. Neither was any other military branch. This was a black ops mission, set up deliberately by unnamed patriots with less than three stars and several civilian leaders, to fish out corrupt military personnel working with civilian counterparts in friendly and non-friendly countries. Nobody wanted to know anything unless there was hard irrefutable evidence to convict. Careers were on the line, and more so, a powder keg was set to explode that could easily erupt into another global war; a thought the central banks frequently drooled over. Central banks never lost money, they win when you lose, and win when you win. They are the ultimate winners of the monopoly game, and continue to lend out money so the game can continue, but only on their terms. Stone would have access to cash and any equipment he required. Stone would also receive additional training and preparation.

A week later, specialists from the Army and Navy arrived to provide Stone asymmetric warfare training, IED development procedures, training for high altitude covert deployment, and in country avoidance; satellite burst transmissions and frequency jamming protocols were taught, as well as the psychology and practice of interrogation. Stone already had the skill sets for sending and receiving coded messages and transmission intercepts. He spoke below average Russian, Turkish, and Greek, and enough Kurdish to scream,

"Don't shoot me; I am too damn pretty to die."

It would be funny enough to provide the edge needed for a hip shot. Finally, Stone certified as a designated marksman for counter-sniper Small Kill Teams. When asked if he would be receiving hand-to-hand combat instruction the specialists laughed and said, "Use your weapon   Rookie, that way you don't break a nail, and always go for the knee first, unless you already have what you came for."

During this extra training, Stone expedited a successful effort to obtain his degrees in Geology and Physics. As part of his extracurricular research, he conducted subsurface investigations prospecting for oil wells. He sold the well prospects to an outside company introduced to him by his visiting professor who was also working in the Middle East and Texas. These efforts became lucrative for Stone while he developed convoluted inroads that also introduced him to a pot beginning to boil involving Iraq, Kuwait, and Iran.

The money from his oil prospecting gave him a considerable nest egg providing additional cover for the cash provided by his handlers: cash a typical Airman would not have. Developing just one oil well prospect made him more money in one week than his entire annual Air Force income. His sports car and once-a-week all expense paid parties were the only luxuries he allowed himself; these were enough to keep his friends and superiors aware that his lifestyle was much different from that of an ordinary Airman. Nevertheless, one in which they all enjoyed participating.

Stone's relationship with his Landlord began to pay off when the local police arrested another Airman on drug possession charges. The request for the Airman's release came with a few bottles of Bourbon and a bag of cash. Predictably, the Landlord was concerned there were no cigarettes with the package. Therefore, his immediate answer was no, but a few drinks later it was determined that Stone could get a key to the jail door and the cell. When the Landlord took his troops for an all expense paid late night dinner, Stone would liberate the criminal.

A few days later, bloodied and with a broken shoulder bone, Patrick was helped out of his jail and driven by military police to the Iraklion Airport to be put into a diplomatic mail pouch and loaded into a waiting C-5. It would not be the last time Patrick and Stone would meet. The episode however solidified Stone's standing with his landlord and opened up opportunities with his "friends" that were not available before. Stone did not mind the deception; he felt it did not compromise his integrity. All he was doing was letting his "friends" continue to use him the same way they had already been doing. Stone's reputation among his military peers as a party hound and someone looking for trouble also took hold. Furthermore, Patrick was grateful for his liberation and removed from his sadistic jailers. Stone would use that appreciation very soon.

Stone did his job well, but there would be a personal price. It was not long before a number of transportation and supply sergeants took notice of Stone and wanted to join the enterprise. They quickly began to discuss multiple opportunities that crossed borders and oceans. Stone had now tied Europe, the Middle East and bases in the United States together with his reputation for excess and his willingness to dabble in business. It was becoming more difficult for Stone to distinguish between who he was, from what he was becoming in the eyes of others. He constantly reminded himself of the differences, while remembering what the philosopher Friedrich Nietzsche wrote, "When you stare into the abyss the abyss stares back at you." Stone must never become that which he seeks to destroy.

On a hot August night, Stone had just returned from a black ops mission known only to his commander and the two handlers now working directly with the Colonel. Fortunately, the mission that was completely off the books had been successful. Meaning he returned alive without leaving any evidence of his presence in another country. He had located the source of a "guns for drugs" operation that had been using military aircraft to transport and distribute illicit products throughout the Middle East, the United States, and Europe. He had solid leads as to where the counterfeit dollars were coming from. He discovered plates for US One Hundred Dollar Bills, and a printing press owned by the Shaw of Iran. Those counterfeit dollars went to a Panamanian drug dealer working with the CIA, called Noriega, to pay off loans given to the CIA, who use the loans to buy guns for Middle East insurgencies. The problem was that the evidence pointed to very high level American government officials, working with leaders of other nations. Counterfeit money printed by the Shaw, was unknowingly laundered by Noriega, then used to purchase guns and ammunition; the guns were traded for drugs, and the drugs were turned into cash, which purchased gold coins. The coins went to the various partners in the organization. These were the blackest of dollars—*Dollars of Death*. At the time, banks never questioned where gold coins came from, only large unexplained volumes of cash. The banks also never saw the string of dead bodies, and young drug addicted children sold into slavery that Stone kept tripping over during his investigation.

Stone began to debrief his base commander at the Officers' Club. The bright moon was lighting up the calm, mirror-smooth Aegean Sea. Stone and the Colonel clicked their tumblers and drank down the smooth, sweet liquor of grapes first fermented then distilled to a brandy unique to the Greek islands, with just a drip of sunshine added to represent a tear from Aphrodite, the goddess of love and beauty. Over the years, the colonel had not only become Stone's mentor, but also a friend. They had developed a strong bond of trust and respect for one another.

Stone reported that one team member in the mission was dead. All six of the Kurds they were meeting with, plus two CIA operatives working with them, were terminated. They were kept alive, however, until Stone and a Navy Seal sniper named Buck, had made sure that every mission goal and every memory known to the bullet-riddled combatants had been wrenched out of them and stored on a tape recording, before they died.

The week before, Stone had located Patrick and called in the favor from Crete. Stone wanted an introduction to a clan of Kurdish terrorists. They were running drugs across the border, in between blowing up tourist buses in Istanbul. Buck, Stone, and Patrick were to fly out to the remote boarder region of Turkey and Iraq, just east of Lake Van, to close a transaction that would also introduce Stone to another top smuggling group. He had been trawling for them over the last 48 months. To Stone, most of the fighters he came into contact with in this region were called terrorists, but were in reality men denied use of their ancestral lands on which they could build homes, raise crops and livestock, love their families, and enjoy their own unique brand of culture. Their type of terror was an attempt to force a compromise allowing them to secure land and to participate in free trade. It was naïve to think diplomacy could work for these people: no decision maker would listen. It had been so for the last three hundred years. The Kurdish people Stone had lived with, were not asking for any other culture to die out or vanish, they just wanted to exist: unlike, the better known terror groups that were pushing their specially twisted brand of religion that forced others to worship a god as they defined his will to be. These perspectives would also serve Stone in later years.

The previous observations aside, Stone had to remember that the Kurds in front of him were capable, and willing to take his head at any moment. Most disturbing, however, was the fact there were two white faces in the group manipulating the Kurds naivety; frantically whispering twisted information into their impressionable ears.

It was partly because of Buck that Stone was still alive, partly because of his partner Patrick, and perhaps because of blind intuition. For sure, the claymore mines that established a kill zone, set prior to meeting, provided a decisive edge to the unintended battle. During a standoff, the Kurds pulled their weapons at the command of the white faces and became aggressive due to questions posed by Stone. He did not want to hand over two million US dollars to a bunch of lackeys and would only do business with their bosses. Perhaps their anger magnified because Stone might have referred to them as goat kissers, instead of lackeys. Again, his Kurdish was really be-low par. It was Buck, hidden in the rocks, who put a bullet in the gunmen's head when he pointed his rifle at Patrick. That gave Stone and Patrick enough time to detonate the clay-mores, and begin to discharge their weapons, which subdued the rest. It was a moment that Stone had trained for, a moment he could never fully recall. When Stone saw one ag-gressors face turn red from the snipers bullet, it was as if he blacked out and something internal took over. There was plen-ty of time; everything lost color; everything turned different shades of white; everything moved in extreme slow motion. Even the lead shot from the claymores seems to freeze in mid-air. When the gunshots were over, the next thing Stone recalled was that his reloaded Colt 45 was in his right hand ready to shoot at any movement on the ground in front of him, and his left hand was on Patrick's chest trying to stop the blood as it gushed out. But it only allowed Stone to feel Patrick's heart beat grow slower and weaker, until the blood stopped flowing completely, and silence took over. There were no tears; no sorrow, it was a warriors death. Patrick, however, did not die for a cause; he died paying back a favor. Patrick had already died back in the Greek jail; he had infringed on the local drug trafficking ring supervised by the police without paying a license fee to sell and distribute. For that, those who were offended by the territorial breach adjudicated a summary execution, in the form of a slow death. His release from jail merely delayed his destiny.

Even after years of preparation intended to keep it from happening, blind rage took over Stone: it was a rookie reac-tion, he hoped to avoid. Yet, Stone, soaked in blood and out of breath, still walked away with the information he came for. Losing a person that you have just begun to know and like, in such a meaningless way was a new lesson for both him and Buck. With everything revealed, even Buck, the seasoned warrior was at a loss when he learned the reason for them be-ing there. It was a crime that one day the bastards would pay for—Stone and Buck both swore this oath.

Stone now knew one of his country's darkest and most senseless secrets, and he was mortified over his government's illegal actions. It was absolute political power run amuck. Another top down initiative that served no one but a few greedy people that convinced someone in authority that these dealings would be good for national security and the nation as a whole. But in reality it was a program that used tax payer dollars for personal gain with no return whatsoever to the nation. The integrity of the few that pay attention was again lost in the arrogance found in the corridors of government corruption. Because an agency could not get the funds they wanted from Congress, the agency decided to go into business on their own. For that, Patrick's body would lay in an unmarked grave on a remote Turkish mountainside overlooking a clear deep blue lake, another soldier unclaimed by his government. The others left on the ground for the ants and vultures.

Back at the Officers Club in Crete, the base commander put down his sniffer of brandy, this old warrior had seen more horror and deception than anyone sane person would want to admit, he lit up a cigar and leaned back in his chair with a distant stare on his face. After hearing the results of the mission from Stone, he said,

"There are three species of people on this earth: shepherds, wolves, and sheep. Eventually everyone must decide which one he or she will become. To ensure your own happiness, you must also make certain which one you are and then match your actions to your choice. You cannot fault others their choice. You simply have to accept the fact that people will be what they choose to be. Most would rather be sheep mechanically paddling neck deep in the thick smelly liquids of ignorance, than have to drain the pool and be aware they are wading barefoot in the stickiness of reality. You have to pick your fights and your battleground. You were lucky this time. The people who sent those wolves have a hell of a lot more to send. More so, agencies rarely go off the reservation without some kind of guidance from the top. I am not going to tell you what to do. I have to keep the tapes. Stone, you are a natural shepherd in wolves' clothing; trust your instincts, they will guide you. I have one last surprise, except for the NASA Astronaut Corps, you choose your next assignment, and it is yours."

The deaths were in vain and the mission was shutdown. The lessons learned concerning the futility of unmanaged government and the senseless deaths that ensue would remain with Stone forever: combined with new perceptions of what constitutes the needs of man, poverty, happiness, liberty, and community.

After his last assignment in the Air Force, Stone went to graduate school and traveled as a consultant. In the years that followed, he opened various business enterprises. Plagued with knowledge of nations and governments, thankfully kept out of public view, Stone was looking to bring meaning back to his life. He wanted to make a difference. His travels showed him squalor, misery, and poverty in one part of the world that had all the resources any other country had. The mystery was, with everything equal, why one country was happy and thriving, while the others were miserable. He concluded the key to the answer must lie in the ability to visualize a common purpose for living and then find the leadership that inspires towards that goal.

Stone worked for over 30 years in environmental science, farming, and researching natural ecosystems. Once he invented a decentralized, sanitation process that he felt would eliminate the need for septic systems and sewer plants and could significantly reduce water consumption in a home. Next, he built centralized systems that multitasked making electricity and producing fertilizers all while treating waste. All companies that he started had one thing in common: they tried to solve significant problems while also separating a person as far as possible from a dependency on any government. But it was always a struggle trying to get the projects off the ground, but he never gave up.

3

Inconceivable Adversity

Even the stench of death and the repression caused by a corrupt government cannot put down poets hidden in the hardened hearts of people wanting to shine in humanities bright light.

Years later, after Stone left the Air Force; a devastating earthquake destroyed Port-au-Prince, Haiti in January 2010, killing over 200,000 people. Buildings became instant piles of rubble, as the ground torn open and folded upward.

In a small area of Port-au-Prince, the back of a huge person turned towards a curious crowd of spectators. Huge arms were flinging blocks of concrete the size of small coffee tables, this way and that way. People just stood back, knowing this digging machine had only one mission, and worrying where blocks of rubble were landing was apparently not a concern.

It took five minutes, but this monster of a man backed out of the burrow he created holding two of his much smaller friends. They were yelling to let them go but he kept on hugging them while tears streaked his black face powdered with the dust from that fatal day. After he had checked to make sure his childhood friends had only scrapes and no crushed bones, they all ran off to help dig out their families and friends.

Standing seven feet two inches and weighing 450 pounds, Pierre, more of a towering bear than a child, is only sixteen years old. His chest was larger than a barrel of water and his arms are as round as a telephone pole. He presents a force to contend with when scared or angered. Nevertheless, when found at ease, he has a soul that even astonishes God. His smile could put you at ease as fast has his anger would make you want to crawl in a hole.

Jacques is a natural born con man, more out of necessity than nature. He is an expert at entertaining you, while he is also emptying your pockets. He is slight, loud when needed, and bright. He is skinny, small, and quick. One minute he is in front of you, but if you blink an eye, he can be gone. He is one of his teacher's quickest studies. Jacques is most devoted to his family and his friends. If you were poor like him, he could always find a moment to help. God never did anything for him but he would be more than happy to attend church if the Ushers would just let the collection plate pass by him…just once. His smile shines, and he is also so very lucky. Just moments before the quake hit, he and Michel had been sitting at a desk studying a school assignment while also giggling at the girls. Then out of nowhere, it seemed the world started to simply fall apart. They were thrown to the floor, and without thinking, they scrambled under the heavy wood table that later saved their lives. The other children were not as lucky.

Pierre was outside the window using a bucket as a urinal when he turned around just in time to see the building collapse on his schoolmates. Michel was dazed, but Jacques' high-pitched voice yelled out to Pierre for help. Without thinking, Pierre did as commanded.

For years, Jacques was the Prince of the Streets. His expertise was finding deals where he and his friends could make some quick money. Their mothers decided what the money they gleaned would purchase. Pierre was their bodyguard; Jacques was the negotiator and businessperson.

Michel was always the enigma. You could hit him or slap him, you could even try to embarrass him, but he would not show the slightest emotion. It was as if he was made of rock. Years of abuse from street thugs and other people of tenuous authority trained him not to react. He is much shorter than Pierre is, but still has a very strong robust frame. Really, it is ridiculous to compare anyone to the size of Pierre. Michel has an internal code of honor that is unbendable, and that attribute makes him immoveable when injustice rears its vicious head. Many times Pierre would have to pick him up kicking and screaming and carry him away from certain death when drug dealers or corrupt police would impose themselves. Nevertheless, unknown to most, existing deep inside of Michel, even with his hardened heart, lived a poet that aches to one day escape and bloom in the light of humanity's highest potential.

All these boys had become men before their time. They were the male heads of their households: the duty forced upon them as it is with most poor families anywhere, the fathers leave all too early.

Michel lived in the street, as did Pierre and Jacques. Their houses were too small for the large families. It was better that their mothers and their small siblings stayed in the homes, where they would stay dry and relatively safe. Michel and his best friends did not mind living outside as long as they had each other. For the most part, everyday was an unexpected adventure.

Normally, every evening they would climb to the relative safety of the flat concrete roof tops; there they could also find a sea breeze and end the day looking at stars while planning out each other's lives just before sleep would overtake them, and dreams of tomorrow would light up their inner worlds. Tonight would be different.

All three were digging into each other's homes, digging towards the crying and screaming. Mothers and their babies were pinned-down by concrete rubble and wood beams. These pathetic structures built by slumlords, only wanted to make easy money, preying on those unfortunate enough to fall within their sphere of influence. Deep inside the rubble, the cries, and screams of Michel's family mingled with the sound of digging.

Pierre was fortunate that his entire family was out when their home imploded. Michel was not so fortunate, and he called to Pierre for help. There was a huge wooden beam sticking out, and lying on top of it was a slab of concrete that was once the roof. Michel could look through the rubble and see his mother holding onto his brothers and sisters.

Pierre put his massive back under the beam and filled his lungs just before heaving the beam upward while he let out a warrior yell intended to wake up Papa Legba, a loa in the Haitian Vodou religion, otherwise known as the guardian of crossroads. A loa is a spirit or lesser entity that can speak directly to the otherwise indifferent Haitian Vodou God, Bondye. As a result, the slab surged upwards, and Michel was able to crawl in and pulled his family towards safety. Pierre was sure Papp Legba helped to put everyone on the proper path—away from immediate death.

Jacques' family was sitting outside their home in a daze. They had dug themselves out. With a quiet composure, he hugged his mother and sisters. They were scared and crying, but safe and well.

The night began to consume the day, but no one could sleep with the moans and muffled screams for help coming out of the rocks and rubble. The next day the boys gathered their families and took them to the park away from the dead bodies that lined the streets. The boys started to look for food and water. The boys spread out to increase their chances. Looters had broken into grocery stores and loaded up with canned goods and water, commodities that were worth more than gold. You could settle a lot of old scores for a can of peas. Trashcans, picked clean of anything that looked like food, littered the side of the roads. The wind caused the balance of the trash to pile up into any nook or cranny.

Michel passed by a massive fissure in the Earth and saw thousands of bodies stacked like cord wood and were beginning to rot in the hot sun. Someone had soaked them with diesel and set the bodies on fire. It seemed the only way; there were no others there to help. Dead bodies meant disease followed by more death. No one would know what had happened to these children, parents, or friends: There were no morgues; there were no records. A nearby pile of wallets and documents, contained identification stripped from the bodies before villagers tossed them in the deep cracks. Spared were Michel's family and friends and for that he gave silent thanks. His thoughts now turned to the following days.

Jacques was able to score some bottles of water, cans of food, and cereals. Pierre found a big bag of rice under a fallen house. Michel found an avocado and a mango tree with fruits not quite ripe but good enough.

With the families fed, now finding a place to fall asleep was priority. Everyone would be facing a long night due to the screams and moans still heard; only slightly muffled by the rock. Pierre, Michel, and Jacques did what they could when they heard someone in the fallen buildings. They were able to dig out many, only to watch them slowly die because there was no medical care. Still, they could not liberate many. In most cases, they could only mark the locations in the hopes that rescue workers with equipment would come soon.

There was horror in everyone's heart knowing that only a few feet away people were dying, simply because there was no way to free them. Convinced that they could do no more, eventually, the three friends gathered their families and started to walk towards the countryside. There they would be able to find water, nuts, and fruits.

More than one and a half million people were now homeless because of the earthquake. There would be more families following in their tracks soon. The boys found an area where others were starting to squat. They gathered wood, plastic, sheets, and cardboard; anything that could be used to create the beginnings of a tent. By the hour, more tents kept springing up, and the grass began to disappear under the thousands of feet pounding the dirt.

The smell of ten thousand people living in close quarters had also started to take a toll. The stench of urine and feces was everywhere. The hormones from urine filled the air and mixed with the heat and humidity. Fights between men would break out seemingly for no reason. Women who traveled to far from a crowd became victims of morally deprived rapists.

All anyone could do was wait to see if help would arrive. Otherwise, the only goal was to survive. The friends had to find more food and water for their families. With their duties completed, they returned to the city to help dig out more bodies so mothers, fathers, and orphans could mourn over their loss.

Meanwhile, butterfly wings that flapped in one part of the world, began to stir the air just enough, so that a storm began to form in another part: a storm that would eventually rain down a torrent of good.

4

Inspired Solutions

With your good health, food on the table and a safe place to sleep, poverty is simply a state of mind. It just means someone else has more toys than you do. Without the essentials, it is a death sentence.

It was September 2009 in Florida. Stone was fighting for the life of his company. An economic meltdown started in the housing markets; the result of wolves in the financial markets and sheep following each other to the slaughter. The result was a loss of trillions of dollars in savings.

The year ended with the greatest equity theft the world could ever imagine and the thieves hid within the vast and unending bureaucracy of government and largest financial institutions. The thieves were screaming foul and pointing accusing fingers at anyone who dared tried to explain what really happened. Hate filled propaganda was generated by the thieves, so the emotionally charged confusion would take the light off of them--clearing the way for their exit as another administration took over. As the thieves walked away with their bounty, many generations of innocent children would have to pay the debt they created.

Stone was at the mercy of investors to keep his company alive. He was close to launching his new invention into the American markets, but that hope hit a brick wall almost overnight.

He was counting on one last push to get units into the hands of his dealers for testing, but his programmer let him down by missing his deadlines, busting his budget, and simply promising more than he could deliver. Old investors were turning on him; new investors were stepping up, but they never sat down to write the required checks. There was too much blood in the water, they knew with time the deal would get better. Grants from the government were as real as the legends of Big Foot. Pessimists kept pissing on any flame that began to grow.

Most disturbing, however, was the fact that the invention could have helped over 3 billion people who currently are without any type of sanitation for their body wastes. Stone new that if a pandemic were to start taking the lives of millions of people, the source of the microbes causing the death would originate from misused pharmaceuticals mixed with human waste exposed in open pits and trenches. A pandemic originating from a source like that would not honor boarders, race, or economic status. That was the 'Why' behind Stone's efforts and inventions.

He deeply enjoyed his work; it was the perfect outlet for his creativity: but for some reason, be it his ego, be it fern fairies, or perhaps the universe's design for his life, destiny kept pushing him towards another direction. Through the years, he realized, as long as things were moving forward with only a few hurdles, he could rest assure that he was on purpose. However, when roadblock, after roadblock kept getting in his way, it surely must mean the Librarian wanted him to take another road.

Perhaps there might have been some sort of Vodou involved in these roadblocks: perhaps someone was calling to Papa Legba to change the course of a few lives, so many more could benefit…perhaps. When it comes down to it, perhaps, a person's troubles has nothing to do with them at all;

perhaps it might be an effort to divert one's attention from self, so they could see and, perhaps, help find ways to relieve the more devastating misery found in the lives of others.

With only 38 dollars in the bank, Stone had to find a solution; it had little to do with economics other than paying his bills, and had everything to do with the reasons for his walking the Earth. That was when the unimaginable happened: Stone's life experiences put him in a unique position to help.

The Haitian earthquake had displaced over a million people in Haiti. It was a situation that would only get worse as families living in makeshift tents strived to stay alive while the rains mixed their waste with mud, making the impossible even more impossible. Then a cholera outbreak began to spread across the island.

Stone had invented a decentralized sanitation system that held promise solving waste management problems in remote areas; it also would create jobs locally in Haiti; but Haiti needed more. Developers were proposing to build cheap housing but that did not solve any long-term issues and addressed very few short-term problems. Haitians needed a complete package that would boost their economy while providing homes with sanitation and electric. They needed a jobs program. They needed economic incentives and investments shielded from political corruption. As well, they needed a program to grow and distribute food in Haiti. The days of children eating dirt cookies must no longer be a part of Haiti's future. The country needed a program that would rebuild it from the bottom up.

A less obvious problem also needed to be addressed— that of doing no harm. Many of the programs, donor groups try to implement, actually do more harm for a nation than good. Some of the programs only make it easier for the local elite to maintain or even gain more control; allowing them to exert even more influence over an already crippled government. Any plan must incorporate a complete understanding of the current government's goals and policies, so "blowback is minimized."

Stone immediately saw an opportunity for Haiti's leaders as well as the international community to rebuild the entire island in a way that corrected many of the past deficiencies. Many others expressed the same viewpoint.

Pondering this, Stone thought back to the days when the first Pilgrims landed in America in 1620. As in present day Haiti, there was no economy. Even the pre-earthquake Haiti had an economy that only benefited the top 20% of the population. How did the American economy grow from a boat dumping a group of people on a beach to what it is today?

The answer seemed simple. The first thing the Pilgrims did was offer thanks to their god for a safe passage. The next thing they did was draw up a contract between them: each person agreeing to do certain tasks for the community. It was the first formal farming cooperative in America. They began hunting and gathering food, and eventually they learned how to grow crops on the new land: everyone shared with each other. Eventually, families moved out of the cooperative to risk life on their own. Soon, people began to trade excess food for other services like help to build a house, or they might trade food or livestock for a plow. The birth of a new capitalist economy began.

From these few simple steps, the economy began to grow. The economy crashed 390 years later because people began to live beyond their means. They fell for marketing ploys that convinced them to buy things they did not need to impress people they did not care about: easy credit made it possible for people to spend more than they could ever possibly earn. Credit made it easier for a person to fall into a bottomless pit from which they could never crawl out.

Fortunately, for Haiti, the world's media turned their cameras on Haiti's challenges, and donations started to flow-in from strangers who wanted to help solve the problem--but there was no program, just a band-aid to heal the symptoms. The cancer was still there.

Globally, in fact, there are over three billion people infected with the same exact cancer and for the same exact reasons. The earthquake was not the problem, it just added to the misery. What the earthquake did for Haiti was to wake up a few sleeping giants.

There were hundreds of contractors and not-for-profits wanting to build homes, but again housing was only a small part of the problem. Building sub-divisions could in fact lead to slums and problems that could fester into even greater challenges in the future.

An effective program needs to address the very basic survival requirements of a population: a program that gives people hope, pride of ownership, jobs, economic growth opportunities, and incentives to keep moving forward. While doing so it would be important that their unique cultures and traditions remain viable. The same program, once proved, could serve other nations.

Stone thought back to the villages of Crete where even in present day terms they lived in what many consider poverty, yet they were very happy people. Even though these Greeks were poor, their streets were clean their fields were trimmed and planted, and smiles donned their sun bronzed faces. With food on the table and a safe place to sleep, poverty was simply a state of mind. It just meant someone else had more toys than you did.

People did not require televisions, high priced tennis shoes, or gold and diamond jewelry to be happy. They needed shelter and the opportunity to grow food and the ability to participate in the fair trade for goods. They needed clean water. They needed freedom to express their viewpoints, safety from injustice of any kind, and liberty. They needed an opportunity to work harder to earn more if they desired.

It seemed to Stone that the other requirement for happiness was a sense of community and belonging. Even though there are high crime rates and corrupt government in Haiti, the bulk of the population survived by helping each other, derived from a sense of community.

The best plan for the islands rapid and successful reconstruction would use Haiti's best attributes, and a bottom up growth model. Quickly, Stone had the fundamentals of such a program in mind. A basic financial analysis indicated it would cost each owner the equivalent of harvesting just nine tomatoes a day to live.

There remained another important problem: Stone could not use his invention for sanitation; because in the best of times, electric in Haiti was expensive and mostly unavailable. A newer less costly method for sanitation was needed. Immediately, Stone saw an opportunity based on new research from universities in England that demonstrated sewage contained between 6 to 17 kilowatts of power per liter of discharge. That was amazing: imagine the accomplishment, to use sewage for power generation, instead of using electricity to treat sewage. Moreover, the technology to do this was not new. It was just a matter of letting the sewage naturally create methane gas and then use that gas to run generators. Using sewer gas to make light and generate heat has been around since the time of the Romans.

Stone began to design methods to economically treat human and farm waste while also generating enough electricity to supply industry and homes. This process would also produce nutrient rich soil amendments for farming, liquid fertilizers, recycled water, and crops that provided renewable raw materials to manufacture paper, textiles, ropes and other value added products. All these raw materials for agriculture, manufacturing, and the residential services that result, all derived from the treatment of sewage, would cost the families less than $0.30 per day; less than one tomato each.

The first step was to find land that was fertile and had a sustainable water supply. Everything else would grow from that.

In the northern part of Haiti, next to the Dominican Republic border, lived a Haitian man. Over the years, he had leased 14,000 hectares of land from the government. There were seven miles of beaches and an inlet from the Atlantic Ocean leading to a bay that was over 100 feet deep. Less than 1000 feet offshore were coral reefs, and after those, the ocean floor dropped to over 2000 feet. Cold nutrient rich waters rose from the depths of the nearby oceanic trench causing blooms of plankton to grow that fed schools of fish that could feed a population.

The entrance to the bay contained old French forts, built before the great slave rebellion. During World War II, hemp and sisal grew on the land near the inlet. After harvesting, the fibers from the plants were manufactured onsite into canvas, rope, and sails, and then sold to the US Navy during the war. The clear waters of the bay were full of seagrass and mangrove that provided nursery grounds for thousands of species of marine fish that the Navy and the locals would also purchase.

South of the bay laid many hectares of unproductive land containing rich volcanic soils that could otherwise support cattle, a dairy, and farm crops. Further south still, were hills, mountains, and valleys long ago stripped of their forests so that families could have charcoal for cooking.

Maurice was a businessperson and a visionary. He had been trying to get investors interested in his property, so a port and new sustainable city could be built that would employ the many people now living in Ft. Liberte' and the surrounding smaller villages. A few years back, the government had spent a small fortune conducting historical and environmental resource surveys of the region, hoping to stimulate economic development.

Maurice was mulatto, one of the mixed blood ruling classes found on the island, raised in the twilight between white and black. Even though he was one of the privileged, he experienced the downward pressures of the elite while enduring the verbal abuses of the many poor that he lived amongst as a child.

Maurice did not see color; he was tired of the ignorance that classified a person's ability based on their race, sex, or economic standing. His vision was to build a city where rich and poor, no matter their race could live together enjoying an island where joy was the primary measure of wealth. A city sandwiched between the deep blue ocean and mountaintops that at times, puffy white clouds seemed to swallow.

A hardnosed lawyer named Mary would soon merge the flowing streams that represent the lives of Stone and Maurice. Mary is a prosecutor in the State of Tennessee. Every Sunday she attended the same church as her dentist. This dentist would go to Ft. Liberte' on a regular basis. He would give free dental care to the people. It was there that the dentist would eventually meet Maurice. They quickly became friends. Mary learned about Stone's desire to help and his plan to build farms in Haiti, so she set about the task of arranging a meeting between Stone and Maurice.

Meanwhile, Stone began to schedule meetings with attorneys and marketing experts in Orlando, Florida, who were his closest friends and confidents to pitch the idea. They were all busy professionals, but never missed an opportunity for a free lunch. The meeting took place in a conference room lined with bookshelves trimmed with polished woods and brass. A long granite top table surrounded by brown leather chairs adorned the center of the room. It was the opulence found in the offices of a successful law firm. These were Stone's friends. The room was full of professional contacts and friends who worked together, so Stone started without introductions.

Pitch of a Lifetime

Instead of desiring to live the American dream, Haitians will work so that the American dream will be to visit Haiti.

Standing next to a large screen, Stone faced his inquisitive audience. He intended to help his peers understand Haiti's history, and then describe what a properly laid out plan could do for its future. He began:

"By 1780, French-owned Haiti produced 40 percent of all the sugar and 60 percent of all the coffee consumed in Europe. Tobacco, indigo, cotton, coffee, mangos, bananas, sugar, cacao, and hemp are a few of the products that have been part of Haiti's economic past.

"A history of slavery, rebellion, war, selfish dictators, and lack of education and foresight destroyed the glory that could have been Haiti's for the taking. If that dismal history is not overturned, Haiti may never realize its potential."

He pointed out that 80 percent of the population lived in poverty and the top-down method of kick starting this economy has not, and will not work here.

"There is too much apathy, ignorance, corruption, and mistrust to overcome with a mere cash infusion."

"Haiti needs a program that empowers the people at the lowest income levels; one that raises their children to become the economic and political leaders of tomorrow. If properly implemented, 80 percent of the population will be working towards economic and political change instead of supporting the current 1% of the wealthy. Instead of desiring to live the American dream, Haitians will work so that the American dream will be to visit Haiti."

Bobby was an attorney with an economics background, "Stone, you are wading into a storm of crap that for the most part, over the past years America played a big role in making happen. You are going up against some big corporations that have an interest in seeing the turmoil continue in Haiti. US Aid buys many goods from US farmers to feed the hungry in Haiti: that has been very lucrative for a few powerful corporations, not the American taxpayer.

"And consider what happened to Aristide when he declared that the island's gold, copper, and aluminum and other natural resources like oil would be used to build schools, hospitals, roads, and infrastructure. To Aristide, those riches belonged to every person in Haiti, not the elite and international corporations. For taking that position, a rebellion ignited, funded by foreign powers that resulting in his exile to Africa. How are you going to work with that?"

Stone nodded his head and said he would be getting to those concerns soon. In an attempt to titillate the group, however, Stone replied, "Bob we cannot ignore the fact that farms in America benefit greatly by supplying cheap rice to Haitians. Those supply contracts, however, only go to politically connected multinational firms, not to the mom and pop farms. Nevertheless, that same cheap rice has caused farms to close in Haiti, forcing otherwise productive families to move to the cities in search of food and work. As for how that benefits American taxpayers, it does not; the cost of rice continues to rise as the national budget for foreign aid likewise escalates out of control. Again, I ask, how does that benefit an American taxpayer in any good way? There is a better plan, one that does not involve political cronyism: one that everyone can benefit from, the rich and the poor equally."

With the stage set and the problems unveiled, Stone proceeded to disclose a high-level description of his program. The talk seemed like a movie cutting from one scene to another, moving from one point to another, the latter laying a foundation for the next, so that a complete picture of the proposal was revealed in a manner that kept the audience asking for more.

"The 9 Tomatoes a Day program is an agriculturally based effort outlining methods to house thousands of families with an average of five people per household. Each family will own its home and a percentage of a farm cooperative; family members must help to operate it and make it profitable. A sense of community and teamwork will be central to the success of this effort. At least one family member needs to work on the farm. The others can work outside the cooperative to diversify their incomes.

"Seed money for the 9 Tomatoes a Day program will be used to build one prototype farming cooperative in the Ft. Liberte' area, located in northern Haiti. The first community will contain 10,000 multi-family dwellings, each of which will house up to five persons. A portion of the profits created by the farming cooperative will build more farms by paying the generosity forward providing more mortgages, farming equipment, utility infrastructure, and food processing plants to new start up farms. The money will roll from one established cooperative to another startup cooperative instead of paying principal back the "lenders." The "loans" will not carry interest. Lenders will realize that their principal returned from sources other than cash, such as carbon credits.

"The vision calls for the farms to be carbon neutral, water wise, organic, and designed to attract eco-tourism by taking advantage of local resources and attractions.

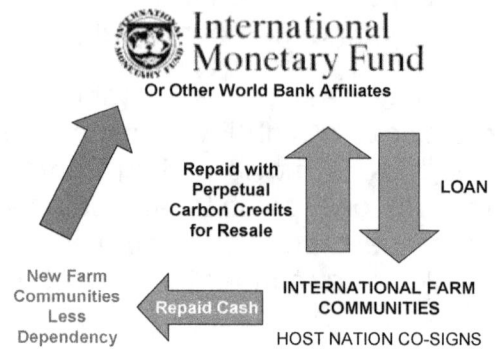

International Monetary Fund
Or Other World Bank Affiliates

Repaid with Perpetual Carbon Credits for Resale

LOAN

New Farm Communities Less Dependency

Repaid Cash

INTERNATIONAL FARM COMMUNITIES

HOST NATION CO-SIGNS

PAY IT FORWARD TO ELIMINATE POVERTY AND DEPENDENCY – One Dollar Solves Multiple Problems

"The farm crops grown will resolve food shortages and provide raw materials that have high value-added prospects for manufacturing. These crops will also result in the sequestering of carbon. A professional team of farming and business experts, employed by the owners/farmers, will manage each cooperative until the residents are trained and certified to take over.

"A new road will connect all the farming cooperatives and will serve to enhance commerce and cooperation between the farming communities spread from the north to the south of Haiti. The road will become Haiti's economic backbone.

"The expected result of funding the 9 Tomatoes a Day Program would be the creation of a worldwide Haitian organic brand and new Haitian businesses that tap into the lucrative global cap and trade initiatives. The farms will raise communities out of poverty and that will stimulate the national economy, while empowering 1,000,000 Haitians with pride of ownership, responsibility, and the desire to be involved in their country's leadership.

"This pride and involvement will flow to the next generation by example of their parents and through education provided by the farming cooperative. The presence of the farming cooperatives will encourage expansion of ports and airports, create manufacturing opportunities, and generate demand for support services. As faith in the new Haitian way of doing business grows, so will investment in their new cities and manufacturing."

The questions began, and the feeling of anticipation started to fill the room. There was some apprehension, the pessimists began to emerge; Stone just ignored them as other eyes started to get wider as thoughts evolved that this program just might work. Box lunches arrived to satisfy growling stomachs. Afterward, Stone would have more ideas and information to offer. Perhaps he could form a team and have a preliminary design charrette.

There would have to be four primary perspectives to consider for any project this size and type. To begin, the opinions of the "first movers," the all-important first ones that would adopt the vision and be instrumental in rallying more support. Next in line the opinions of the Haitian government, and how they want foreign nationals involved with growth in their nation. Then, and most important, are the opinions of the people that will live in the community and what they want for their futures. Finally, the views of the international agencies and donors require consideration, because they will ultimately fund the project.

They Ask for More

Farm cooperatives overcome the curse of smallness while countervailing nefarious market forces.

Stone wanted to get his point across that a robust economy must have agriculture and manufacturing at its core in order to achieve sustainability. Furthermore, all thriving economies have *renewable raw materials* feeding the supply chains for manufacturing operations. Without that, economic bubbles threaten stability. Just building subdivisions would be exactly like scratching an open sore until it becomes infected.

Everyone working in the community had to work towards a common community goal and vision. By doing so, they would be helping themselves and their family, as well as the other community members. These were the founding principles written down and signed, in 1620, by all the members of the first group of Pilgrims that endured a treacherous trip across the ocean in the Mayflower: the first group of new Americans. The Native Americans, who had already occupied the New World for thousands of years instinctively knew and practiced the benefits of cooperation.

Some debate ensued, mostly around words that ended with an ism. Stone deflected most of that talk by illuminating the fact that capitalism also ends with an ism. "We are grown-ups now," Stone insisted. "We know mostly what works and what does not. We also know that there is no one size fits all economic models. The global economy will ultimately be a blend of various models adapted to ideologies, local resources, and capabilities. McCarthyism is dead and buried, and the shameful fear mongering that exemplified his political ambitions if buried with his unmissed rotting bones. Let us keep it that way. My biggest point being on the matter of communities cooperating to achieve a common goal, "...when you are fighting against guns and knives, and all you have is a feather; statistically speaking, there is a better chance of walking away if you have a lot more feathers around you: there is strength in numbers."

"Bobby," Stone began, alerting him it was time to open his eyes, "The 9 Tomatoes a Day program builds farm and marketing cooperatives designed to maximize benefits to the farmer/owners and to build countervailing market power to oppose external factors that would tend to keep the farmer/owners in poverty. Worldwide these nefarious forces have repeatedly stripped away a country's natural resources, burdened the country with heavy debt, and given loans to governments that never made its way down to benefit the poor. The result has been devastating poverty and increased dependency on foreign aid.

"Recently aid given to developing nations has had adverse consequences for farmers. For instance, US Aid offers genetically altered seeds to farmers at no cost. The result is the farmers must continue to purchase seed from the suppliers because the plants they yield are sterile. The fact that the farm will be dependent on an outside seed source forever, must be weighed against a higher more reliable yield and less problems with pests. In addition, what would happen if the seed supplier decided to go out of business?

"The cooperative overcomes the curse of 'smallness.' A cooperative empowers pride of home and business ownership, creates buying power, enhances political voice, and establishes market presence. When multiple cooperatives combine their efforts, they protect the diversity and health of seed stocks and diminish dependency of large suppliers that seek profit over humanity; good foreign policy, and good farm management are by products. The global economy and the environment are the better for this.

"As more cooperatives become operational and begin to work together, a much larger market presence becomes apparent. Economic, political, and social stability are also by-products. Strong business and social leadership, and participation in education by the farmers are crucial criteria in the early stages of any cooperative that builds momentum. The recruitment grounds of terrorists go away because the youth are too busy working to build a future for themselves and their families.

"Cooperatives operate on land donated by the government. The governing by-laws of the cooperatives are in the best interest of the future farmer/owners compiled under the laws of the host country. The governments defer taxes until all international loans or grants requiring "forward payments" have been satisfied.

"The management team will build a business plan that is suitable for the locality and is adapted for the regional climate and soil conditions.

"Potential farmer/owners must successfully pass an interview. The selection process will assess their ability to contribute to the success of the enterprise. The farmers must build each other's homes and the cooperative infrastructure. They only receive food, medical care, and a tent to live in for their efforts until home construction is complete and the food crops begin to generate cash flow. While the parents are working, children go to daycare or school.

"When the crops are ripe, everyone in the community joins in the harvest. If the farm is properly designed and operated, it is likely the <u>equivalent</u> of harvesting just nine tomatoes a day selling at just $0.15 USD each, is all that is needed for a farmer to pay their portion of the farm debt: of course this is only a minimum." Stone put the last slide up on the screen and at the same time passed out a sheet of paper with Table 1 printed on it. The slide showed the projected costs. Bobby looked it over and slowly nodded his head saying, not in total agreement, "It is a start."

TABLE 1: PROJECTED COSTS

			Costs Per Home		
			Year	Month	Day
Price of Land	Donated		USD		
Price of Processing Plants	3,000,000	30 yr	10.00		
Price of Bio Digester	1,500,000	30 yr	5.00		
Cost of Farm and Earth Moving Equipment	2,000,000	30 yr	6.67		
Fuel and Maintenance Costs	500,000	yr	50.00		
Seeds and Animal Costs	500,000	yr	50.00		
Home Cost	9,000	30 yr	300.00		
Misc Overhead	2,500,000	yr	250.00		
Administration	500,000	yr	50.00		
Collateral: Land, Equipment, Structures					
Interest Rate	0				
Years to pay back loans	30				
Number of Homes	10,000				
Debt per Household(USD)			721.67	60.14	2.00
Price of Tomatoes	$ 0.30				
Tomatoes Sold to Pay Costs			2405.56	200.46	6.68

"Yes, Bobby, it is still conceptual—a start. Some items need more funding while others items need redacting; but it is a start. Note also that I left about three and a quarter tomatoes in the field--just in case. Nine tomatoes just sounded luckier than 6.68. At the high end, I see an investment of $21,900 per family of five for a 10,000 family community. Economies of scale play an important part in this program. That payback over 30 years would be less than $2.00 USD a day per family."

Stone went on to reveal how the money was to flow. "When profits are realized by the cooperative, a portion is used to pay forward and build other cooperatives, some is set aside for working capital, and the balance is distributed to the owners as a dividend. Farmers living outside the cooperative can sell their harvest to the cooperative. The income stream resulting from the resale will also benefit the owners. When dividends are paid to owners that is when we can begin to declare success."

Stone stated with a smile, "There is a saying in Creole, 'Tout moun gen yon mouchwa nan peyi,' or 'Everyone has a handkerchief of land.' If we can get them to combine all that land into one cooperative then everyone could own a 'handkerchief' of a big business that helps them get more out of their work. There is power in numbers.

"A typical farm would contain at least 5000 acres and up to 10,000 acres: Approximately one-half to one acre per family; 640 acres would be reserved for housing. A typical dwelling would be 450 square feet with two bedrooms and one bath. It would be part of a quadraplex with a wrap-around porch."

"People can earn more, and have more than others, just like in capitalist societies but the cooperative will make sure that everyone, as long as they contribute to the farm work, has the same basic necessities distributed equally: no matter what the economy looks like outside of the buffer created by the cooperative. This is what I call 'Shock Buffer Economic Design.'

"Sanitation would be provided by mixed plug flow anaerobic digesters. They turn toilet and farm waste into power, fuel, and fertilizers. The gray water in the home that results from washing cloths and taking showers is sanitized and reclaimed in a special unit before it leaves the home and is then used to flush the toilets; or, to grow fish crops, and finally to irrigate cash crops.

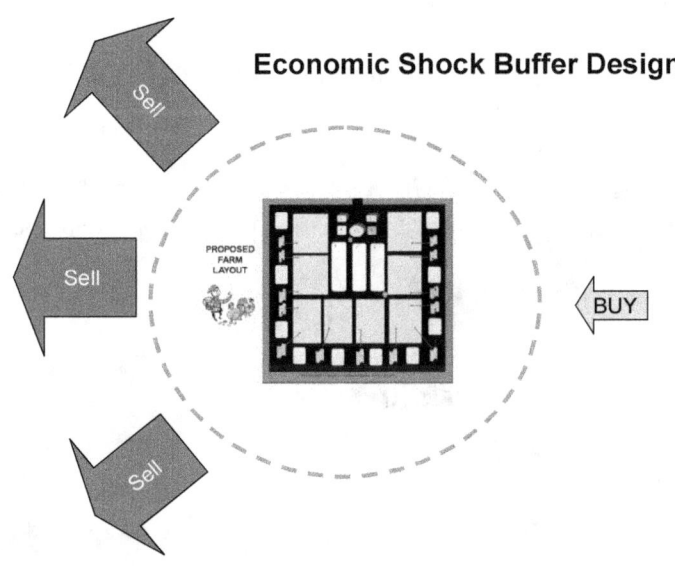

Economic Shock Buffer Design

Sue, a marketing and advertising consultant, slapped the table. "How in the hell can they get a home for that little of money? I paid over $100,000 for my little home and it is in foreclosure because I lost my job."

Stone flinched, said he was sorry, and knew exactly what she was going through. "Sue," he said, "First, the land is donated. Second, these homes will have no frills. They have walls, a roof, windows, doors, and window screens. Finally, owners are responsible for building their homes and all the others. There are no labor costs. Everyone has to work together."

Sue understood but continued to shake her head: more so, from frustration in her personal life, perhaps a little from how much sense cooperatives would make as a standard way of living in America.

ANAEROBIC DIGESTER

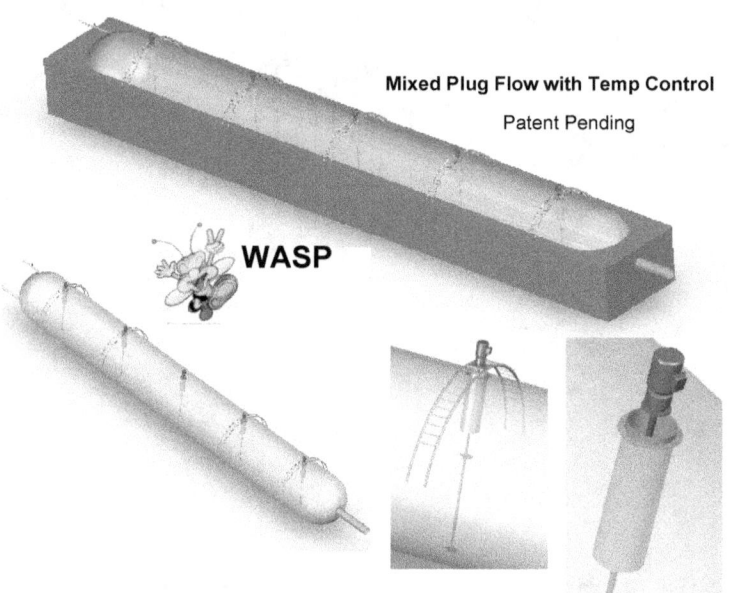

Mixed Plug Flow with Temp Control

Patent Pending

WASP

There certainly was a little jealousy because of the opportunities in Haiti. A chance to create a new sustainable nation based on sound principals that also protect natural resources. Her nation started the same way 390 years ago, before "progress" took over, and political will diminished and methods that are more "efficient" started to kill aquatic and terrestrial life, and to poison the groundwater.

Robert, a CPA and Attorney inquired, "Aren't you concerned that you are promoting commun-'ism' in Haiti?"

And there it was again, another 'ism'. Stone's head and shoulders dropped a little as his eyes began to cross in an attempt to contain his frustration at the question.

"We have been here before Robert. I have no concern at all, but I am concerned about a revival of McCarthyism lead by those who otherwise should be intellectuals," replied Stone.

"We are not Republicans or Democrats running for office here, we are trying to build an economy that works for a group of people that do not have the resources Americans enjoy. Haitians and the other poor have to pool their talents, muscles, and brains just to survive day to day: if that is communism then ok, call it what you want.

"Robert isn't it time we lose the cold war arrogance and work with what we know needs to be done, instead of trying to force political ideas on a group of impoverished people; ideas that we know will fail without the proper infrastructure and leadership?

"Capitalism requires cash, Haitians have none. Cooperatives use labor they have plenty of that. Moreover, what makes you think a cooperative cannot be managed democratically? People can be capitalistic in a cooperative. It happens every day in farming and manufacturing cooperatives across America today. They just cannot go about destroying others, or their community while doing it. No one person is allowed to dominate the monopoly board. Now wait a minute, seems in America there are laws that say that same thing! Does that make Americans closet communists?

"In fact, haven't you noticed America is a socialist government with a capitalistic economy? For the most part so is China. China just has a more centralize government and they control the media. In America, we have just a few capitalists who control the media and what the people get to hear. I am sorry to be short Robert. Nevertheless, with all the education and experience that abounds in America, it frustrates me that the propaganda used in the fifties and sixties to create fear that justified wars in Korea and Vietnam, and to assassinate democratically elected leaders like Patrice Lumumba, still permeates our society today, and keeps us from using social models that promote cooperation amongst community members.

"Let me repeat, the idea of cooperatives has been in existence in America since the days of our founders. Our very first villages were cooperatives: out of necessity, they had to be. Amana was America's largest and most successful cooperative that existed for over 200 years. They split up only because the younger generation did not want to continue the farming traditions while having to pray 11 times a week and wear the same clothing as the others. That, importantly, is a good point to magnify here, as far as I can tell, most cooperatives that failed did so because of poor management or because of their attempts to force beliefs, uniformity and pious lifestyles on the members. They ignored humanities need for individuality, creativity, and rewards while begin part of a larger group for safety. The conundrum here is that the same structured lifestyles imposed on the community by the Amana leaders, which kept the farm successful for so long, ultimately was their downfall. They refused to be flexible and adapt to changing times and perspectives. Those lessons will not be lost here."

Robert heard what Stone was saying and somewhat agreed. However, the years of unchallenged fear and hate filled propaganda fed to him by television, magazines, and his government was too deeply ingrained. Robert was conservative, he did not like change. Ultimately, Stone would have to frame the cooperative in another light, change some words around. Then everything would be fine.

He did not dwell, instead he gave everyone another handout.

"Exhibit One illustrates the multiple paths and uses of one gallon of water. One gallon of water enters the home for cooking and cleaning. Afterwards, it flushes the toilets. The black water flows to the anaerobic digesters. The gray water discharged flows into green houses that captures the vapor transpired by the plants and recycles it before the excess flows into vegetated ponds to grow fish. These fish can feed people or used to supplement the diet of livestock. Then the flow continues to irrigate the cash crops, and finally seeps through the ground towards the rim ditch where more fish are also cultivated.

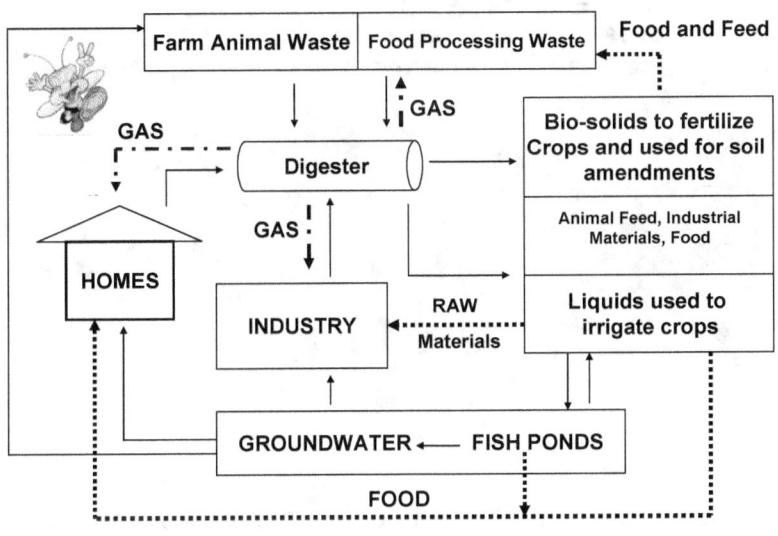

WASP ENGINEERING--WATER, PRODUCTION, and WASTE FLOW

"The discharge will then exit the farm by flowing through sugar cane, Kenaf, bamboo, or hemp fields. These plants will do a final polish of the water while producing yet another type of cash crop.

"Let me give you a brief idea of the value some of these plants can yield. Kenaf is a member of the Malvaceae (mallow) family. These plants feed livestock, provide food and oils for humans, and can yield hundreds of other commercial products like paper, textiles, or rope. It grows in almost any soil and needs little water. Unlike cotton, it requires very little pesticides because of its resistance to bugs. When used in commercial products, it locks up carbon dioxide stripped from the atmosphere during photosynthesis. Additionally, all the products manufactured from them can be recycled numerous times. That means more raw materials for exports and less waste in a landfill."

Sequestering carbon
creates jobs, reduces global warming gases, and increases market competition

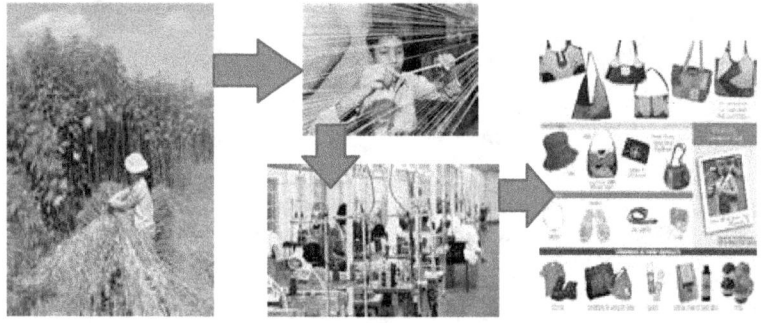

Robert asked if Stone could explain Cap and Trade as well as how carbon credits work. As Stone sketched a few graphs on the white board, he explained that governments set a limit for CO2 and other pollutants a company can discharge into the atmosphere. If they exceed that limit, they have to pay a fine; or, they can purchase carbon credits from someone else that is producing fewer emissions, or from someone that provides a service that sequesters carbon like planting trees, pumping CO2 into the ground for storage, or doing other things like those that we are talking about here in this meeting. Robert acknowledged the answer and Stone moved on.

Stone's final handout was Exhibit 2 that showed the layout of a typical farm. He continued to explain more details:

Exhibit Two: Typical Layout of a 5000 Acre Sustainable Farming Cooperative

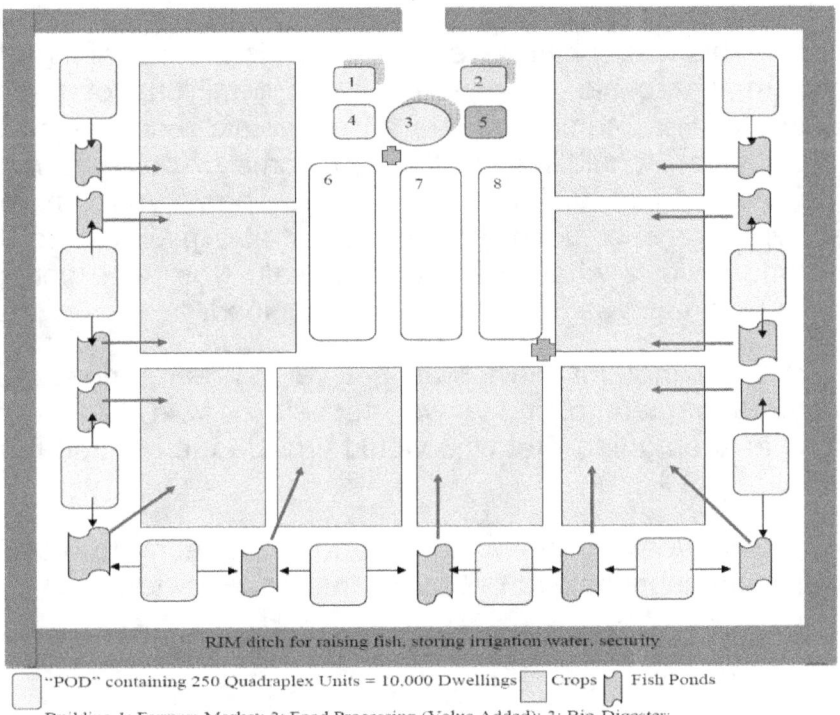

RIM ditch for raising fish, storing irrigation water, security

"POD" containing 250 Quadraplex Units = 10,000 Dwellings   Crops   Fish Ponds

Building 1: Farmers Market; 2: Food Processing (Value Added); 3: Bio-Digester; 4: Dairy; 5: Slaughter House; 6: Dairy Cows; 7: Pigs 8: Chicken/Rabbit/etc

"All landscaping will serve some financial or agricultural purpose. Ornamental flowering plants will support a honeybee or hummingbird population that helps in the pollination cycles of the cash crops. Trees will landscape the sides of roadways. The trees will sequester carbon and yield fruits or nuts.

"Because of the logistics of managing 10,000 partners who have little trust and even less education, a unique program has to be designed that gives a voice to the owners but also reduces the problems that will be faced by management. For instance, each POD will elect three representatives. These representatives carry forward the votes or decisions of their respective POD when it comes to implementing the rules and bylaws that will govern the cooperative. The three representatives also hold court for dispute resolution. These representatives are elders who have earned the respect of the community through their work and contributions.

"This was a high-level view, but it is the beginning of a program that could change the lives of millions of people worldwide. Haiti could become an economic recovery model that if proven, could relieve the symptoms of poverty worldwide, all for just 9 Tomatoes a Day. Thank you for your patience. I have a technical document that explains more details and reviews what I have already said; you need only go to www.9Tomatoesaday.com for the download. "

Even thought there was not yet full agreement most everyone wanted to find a way to help, it was enough for Stone to keep going. But who would provide the needed funding?

In a week, there would be another meeting to discuss funding concepts held at Bobby's conference center.

7

Bringing in the Jack

The fundamental "WHY" behind 9 Tomatoes a Day is to stop pouring money into band-aid solutions for a problem and to start building sustainable solutions that will also rejuvenate the entire global economy; and to begin building a peace that up to now, was only given lip service.

Stone could hear his old lieutenant once again invading his thoughts, "Any asshole can think of a problem, *Start Finding Solutions!*"

"Pessimists can suck lemons as far as I am concerned." Stone thought to himself.

For the last week, Stone had been building spreadsheets showing financial models that would help bridge perceptions of value, prejudices, and self-interest. He was thinking everyone wants to help, but they have families and bills; they need to live, and they do not want to sacrifice the lifestyles they have worked to build. They can work for less, but they still need to be paid. Just then, Bob Marley's singing interrupted Stone's thoughts, "Don't worry about a thing, cause every little thing gonna be alright..." The phone was ringing pulling Stone abruptly pulled back to the present.

TJ Hood was at the other end of the phone call. "Mr. Richards this is TJ." He was being familiar: of course, everyone knew his name. "Robert and I were having lunch and he just described your program for farms and how you thought eco-tourism would help to diversify their income stream."

Stone replied, "I'm surprised Robert dared to use any word ending with an 'ism'."

TJ laughed aloud, "Yeah, he told me not to bring that up, he said how it would set you off."

"Can we get together to discuss the project and some options?" TJ asked. Of course, Stone agreed. Who would turn down a meeting with the number one golfer in the world, despite the past slow sinking of his ratings? Stone invited him to the meeting with all the previous attendees.

Once again, a confluence of troubles continued to mingle with the river of opportunity flowing in Haiti's direction.

The next day, Stone got everyone seated in the same conference room they met in last week. He started his talk about funding opportunities. Most involved money already spent by corporations on mindless advertising or entertainment. The alternative was to redirect the money towards entertainment or advertising driven by purpose. At that moment, Barbara's stomach started to growl so loud, it almost sounded like a muffled fart. This reminded her to ask if anyone ordered lunch. Then TJ walked in.

Everyone's eyes shifted from TJ back to Stone looking for a reaction. Robert leaned over towards the red-faced Barbara and began fanning a piece of paper as if to remove a stink from the general region. She grabbed the paper and tried to compose herself.

Stone casually introduced TJ to everyone at the table. He suggested that any bodily noises emitted from the other side of the table should be ignored. TJ laughed and said, "You just got to love a good fart shared with friends."

Barbara screeched, "It was my stomach growling." Everyone just nodded his or her head in compliance.

Stone felt the room energize a bit simply because TJ took the time to show his interest. Stone continued.

"Beginning this program will be challenging," He asserted, "But it also promises to be the most fulfilling work you have ever done. The footprints of all involved will be deep, significant, and meaningful. Ten communities (PODS) occupy this first farm with 1000 families and homes (250 Quadraplexes) per POD.

"To start, I suggest that we find a way to produce a reality game show casted by at least ten A-list actors and celebrities. Execution and funding of this plan would look something like this: First, a producer, and director will be located, and then 10 celebrities willing to participate in a purpose-based reality program.

"Then the program would be pitched to sponsors. Some funding might come from the US Department of Energy, US AID, and other not-for-profit groups. Most should come from corporate sponsors that would benefit from the expansion of a global market fueled by new homeowners with increased buying power.

"For instance, Home Depot and Lowes could set up programs to help by selling to the farms at cost and then shipping the building materials to the farms. Alternatively, they could commit to donate one 2x4 to the farm for every five sold. When there are successful farms built and villages begin to spring up around them, Home Depot and Lowes would already have brand recognition and good community standing should they decide to enter the market.

"One challenge would be for each celebrity to form a team that would interview, select, and relocate 1000 families each to an area on the farm where a tent city would be erected.

"Before that however, bathhouses, medical and food facilities would need to be setup. Next, land would have to be cleared and prepared for crops. Then the construction of homes would begin. The first team to get all the farmers into homes and their harvest to market would win the challenge.

The celebrities' primary tasks would be:

- To be coaches helping to inspire their teams and help them understand the overall community goals, which might be difficult for some to understand at first.

- To bring in donations such as farm equipment, expertise, seeds, livestock, building materials, and money.

- To organize and motivate team leaders who will schedule and execute the plan.

- To inspire the new farmer/owners.

- To popularize the mission statement.

Ideas such as 9 Tomatoes a Day require funding just to get them recognized. Proposals are rarely read, more rarely funded. However, imagine if we created a reality show and a blockbuster movie based on that show. One that described an important journey; one that embodies all the trials, tribulations, and behind the scenes wrangling that took place, as the skin and bones of the project emerged; then, not only would there be a blockbuster movie making a profit, but a portion of that profit could go towards creating future farm projects.

"The farm that this game show and movie would be based on would also be supported by international agencies and sponsors, but more so through a reality based game show whereby millions of viewers would text in donations.

"The message would immediately spread around the world telling people about the proposal, and viewers could see the immediate results of their donations and support. Moreover, instead of mindless advertising, viewers would see how sponsors use their advertising dollars to make the world a better place for everyone. Vision becomes reality through purpose-based entertainment."

TJ asked if anyone considered building a golf course on the project. "Not to flaunt an ism in Robert's and Stone's faces, but if eco-tourism is to be a major part of the business model can I help to design it?" It did not take long, perhaps four milliseconds, for everyone to agree that TJ could handle the eco-tourism design aspects.

This would be Jack Power's second time attending one of Stone's presentations. Jack is a well-known entertainment attorney with far reaching connections on both coasts. The fact that TJ even took the time to show up, impressed him. He saw a lot of work ahead, but a reality-based show funding the building of a farm cooperative and a feature film was a new slant. Jack knew the basic marketing principal that people buy *"why"* you do something, not *what* you do.

The fundamental *"why"* behind the 9 Tomatoes a Day program was solid and it rang true to everyone he talked to about it from the previous week. To build farms that improves the quality of life for everyone on the planet. Jack remained sold on the concept as he went about calling his contacts to help develop the first group of contestants. From his point of view, if the celebrity contestants agreed first to participate, producers, directors, and a syndicator would be easy to enlist.

His first calls were to actors who could bring in their friends and other celebrities. No one was surprised when Sean Glenn was the first to jump on-board. Matt Ramon committed and overnight brought in Ben Ackleff, George Rooney, and Brad Kitt. Remy Moore heard about the event from Glenn and called Jack. Tom Banks agreed, as did Jimmy Muffet and Bill Smith. Sean Donnelly called and offered to help on behalf of the Queen. Forrest Whittier volunteered when he heard of the casting call. This was the first team of coaches.

A star-filled event was taking shape that would eventually fill every living room with people watching their favorite heroes help create a new form of giving that would change the world and the global economy: this was 'Extreme Makeover' on steroids, but on a global basis. The human and logistic struggles would be monumental. Millions of people will watch as thousands of families leave their lives of poverty and misery behind. This was not just one home that served one family; this was the construction of an entire city serving thousands of families. All built in front of a viewing audience.

A month later, the cast members assembled in Orlando for briefing: and to formalize their commitment. Stone waited for the other shoe to drop. He had ideas in the past that had come together quickly only to crash for reasons you could always predict, but worked hard trying to prevent from happening. The program and the commitments from many people offering to help build this farm and to produce the reality show were coming together at lightening speed; all anyone could do was complete the part they agreed to play, and then hold on.

Jack agreed to set up the corporation and to help find a distributor, and more financing. The celebrity coaches analyzed the challenges and the mission statement. They all agreed with the mission and committed their time and effort. They all left with their first goal being to find and organize a team that would also commit to 12 months in Haiti to build the first farming cooperative.

Jack called a friend, Sunny, who had recently been laid-off when the show he helped to manage went off the air. Sunny agreed to produce and film the events as they began to unfold.

Imagine the look on the manager's face, even the members, at the Windermere Golf Club when TJ brought everyone for a round of golf. It did not take long for the Paparazzi to leak what was happening and why all these A-List celebrities were playing golf together. The idea of the reality show became public very quickly and the bidding war for the rights to air it began. Jack's job became very easy.

Stone remembered the third great lesson in his life: be careful what you wish for; you just might get it. He had certainly stepped in it, and it went up to his neck very quickly. The first thing he did was to schedule a flight to Haiti in order to meet with the Prime Minister and to scout out the first farm site. The second thing he did was to set up a factory to manufacture the anaerobic digesters: he also rehired the 200 employees he laid off just 24 months ago.

With the manufacturing contract complete, Stone could now fly to Haiti and concentrate on the farming layout and the negotiations with the Haitian government.

Ft. Liberte' site survey

Purpose is wonderful but politics is reality. Many people may join for a common purpose, but knowing the individuals underlying reasons for doing so is paramount for success.

Stone drove to Ft. Lauderdale and boarded a flight to Cape Haitian. There Maurice picked him up and began to drive east along the coast towards Ft. Liberte'.

Maurice and Stone had met before in Florida. Mary, the Tennessee attorney, also flew into town so she could attend the meeting. Maurice brought with him, his articulate Haitian nephew who was also an American citizen with a Master of Business Administration degree.

After the meeting, that lasted three hours, Stone could only wonder with all the bright and intellectual individuals that swell the Haitian ranks, what exactly was holding back the economic development of the country?

Maurice wanted to build a modern sustainable business center, industrial park, and international port of call with housing for the workers and for retirees that might relocate from around the world who were looking for an easygoing Caribbean lifestyle.

Stone liked that vision, but he also felt a separate farm was needed that would be buffered from any outside economic shocks that the poor are not trained or equipped to deal with. There is a reason in nature a monoculture is rarely found. That is, a monoculture is weak, while a diverse ecosystem is robust. A diverse ecosystem has many more unique niches for species to utilize and become specialists within. It is the same for economies. The more diverse an economy is, the more robust it becomes. Having a farm economy shielded from external economic pressures not only reduces financial risk for the residents, it also helps provide stability for trading partners outside the economic walls of the farm.

For other economic reasons, Stone wanted to reforest the mountains to help restore a normal rain cycle: this would stop sediments from eroding into the bays that killed seagrass, essential for the growth of marine fisheries. With more forests comes wildlife that is more indigenous. This diversity will attract more eco-tourism.

Stone believed in the principle that everything entangles with everything else—it is an immutable law of nature. Every decision man makes that changes natural systems, has a consequence down the treacherous switch backs found on life's mountainous roadways. The idea is to keep life between the lines, and do not ignore the signals that your vehicle is providing.

Haiti is a text book example of how positive feed back systems work, you make one small mistake and that small mistake keeps compounding like interest charges on a credit card: but it doesn't stop there because bigger mistakes are made that add more charges to the balance while the interest continues to add up at an even faster rate. The only way to stop the run-a-way loop is to break the cycle and change the behavior: Repair what damage you can and then return to the basics.

The Earth, for the most part, is self-healing; like a wound heals itself on all living things. That healing process also has foundations rooted in feed back systems. To heal Haiti's environmental wounds, at least in the area of Ft. Liberte', all that is needed is to contain the pollution that enters the bay that currently destroys the marine life; and then re-plant landscapes in a way that water and nutrient cycles once again find their balance.

To break-up the feedback loops keeping the people of Haiti in poverty, the cancer that causes corruption must be cut out. Those causes, then judiciously replaced with programs designed to break the vicious cycles that cause despair. In-spired leaders able to show the people a vision must grow those programs; a program with a common purpose towards which everyone can jointly work.

In better economic times, the project's potential was there; beautiful coral reefs, seven miles of sandy beach, and a protected bay for deep-water yachts and a fishing fleet. Old French forts lined the entrance with unique historical struct-ures. These would offer world class shopping, dining, and nightclub experiences for cruise ships and jet setters. How-ever, as with the American Pilgrims, the basics came first: sus-tainable farms required housing for workers and a steady supply of food, plus raw materials that could support manufacturing and the creation of more jobs. The two projects, Maurice's vision for a sustainable city and the farm inter-locked, mostly due to the current economic times and Haiti's unenviable history of kidnappings, murder, and corruption. Be-fore either vision would see the light of day, a contract, or a declaration of purpose, must be drawn up for the cooperative; one that all the workers/owners could agree to support and agree to be governed by; and one that the Haitian government would publically endorse in front of an international audience of donors.

Attitudes and global perceptions had to change before Maurice's new city or the farm would materialize: a modern sustainable farm managed by vibrant and benevolent visionaries, confirmed and advertized over the airwaves, would herald a new beginning that might encourage new investment for Maurice's dream. First, the Haitian government would have to establish a zone, free of corrupt officials and the tyranny of a few families that maintain the notion that the entire island and its resources belong to them. The new city would have to have its own police force that would protect foreign investment and the people for who they work.

During the drive, Maurice continued to express his concern that the farm would degrade the landscape and become a slum, making the dream of his new city harder to make happen. How could Stone's vision for the farming cooperative dispel that concern?

They were just arriving at the gateway to Ft. Liberte' when a helicopter flew by and turned around to land on the road in front of them. Out came a big toothy smile followed by TJ. There had not been enough time, during the short trip, for Stone to explain the progress since their first meeting; and who would be helping.

During a sit down meeting at a small café, Stone and TJ presented to Maurice a detailed plan for a self-contained farming community. It would be designed eco-friendly and based on the commercial successes of the Napa Valley in California. A place you would want to visit to sample the exotic Caribbean foods, rums and fruits, to bike through the trails lined on both sides with organically grown crops, and then hike up the mountainsides to look over a great vision of the new farm called Hope. A vision that one day could become a model for lifting others out of poverty. The sustainable ideas and new technologies not tried elsewhere would attract developers, builders, governments, and the curious.

Old style bed and breakfast motels with garden dining would be available for buyers, tourists, and entrepreneurs from other countries wanting to learn how the cooperatives operate. The farm would be one of many must-see destinations when visitors come to the Ft. Liberte' wonderland.

A TJ HOOD golf course would be front and center. From the air, the fairways would spell 'ESPWA', a Creole word for hope. Kiosks and cafes would line the walking trails serving fresh rum drinks and exotic desserts all created from cocoa, bananas, and vanillas all harvested just hours before.

FARMERS MARKET MALL AND ENTERTAINMENT CENTERS

ADVENTURE
Well designed farms can be ecotourism destinations

As TJ spoke, Stone watched as Maurice's diffident scowl gradually gave way to slow nods of comprehension and finally to a broad smile of approval. One more very large obstacle to the plan evaporated. Maurice visualized the entire combined community…the merging of individual visions began to form into a common purpose.

Local Farmer Interviews

Electricity attracts the wrong class of people to an otherwise very nice community.

The advance team hired Janet, a local interpreter whose time divided, as needed, between the United Nations and various non-governmental agencies. Janet was French born. Her long black hair, poise, and mesmerizing green eyes caused her to stand out in any crowd. When she turned and smiled at Stone, he would invariably lose his train of thought. She was going to be trouble for someone, he thought. Stone was the first to pick her up, so she could translate during this first survey. They spent a few hours driving through the local villages until it was time to meet up with the other team members.

Bill Smith also wanted to see the farm site and to learn about the people; so he arranged to have TJ pick him up in Cape Haitian, then fly him back to where everyone agreed to join up in a hamlet called Malfety; located south of Ft. Liberte'. From there the real effort began to understand the needs of the region.

Anywhere the group saw workers they stopped to talk and to ask about their greatest needs. Questions flowed like,

"If the impossible could happen, what did they want it to be? What did they need most to help improve their lives?"

The group learned that the ground would support almost any crop, but it was hard and rocky. The farmers needed machines to help plow. Besides the fact it would otherwise take a lifetime of savings to purchase a tractor; in times past, it was not worth the expense and risk because of low market prices. The Haitian farmers were competing against free food provided by aid groups, or imported food with prices subsidized by the United States and European governments.

While the others in the group moved on, Stone lagged behind to ask the more astute villagers questions strategic for the farm's success. Questions like: In practice, what is the Government's goal for use of their land? Who influences government decisions in this area? What are their goals? What industries do they own? Who is impacted by their successes and failures? What companies have been coming around prospecting for minerals or oil? Who controls imports and exports in this area? All questions that if not answered and explored completely could result in an unexpected brick wall. All these questions could lead to early allies or enemies later on.

Later in the day while sitting at a café with a small group of farmers, Bill asked them if electricity would help to improve their lives. An older man that Bill later described as having more wrinkles than a mastiff replied, "I always felt it would attract the wrong class of people." Everyone laughed. Bill stop laughing when he saw the man was looking straight at him; apparently, even without radio or television, stories about Hollywood celebrities can reach remote villages like this one.

Everyone shared ideas, while Janet would translate. The discussion included how the farming cooperative would help them get more out of their work and better prices for their harvest, but mostly how new jobs would become available because of the expanded cash flows, and the opportunities for manufacturers.

There were many skeptical residents and they wanted to know what the Ameriken fe' gooders (American do-gooders) wanted for their efforts. After years of deception and cruelty, it was difficult for the villagers to accept that a group of strangers simply wanted to help a nation rebuild itself: and if not a nation, perhaps just this small corner of a country that establishes an example of what could be.

Sure, everyone had bills to pay, and no one wanted to come out of pocket with cash. However, all the Americans sitting at the table, assumed salaries would evolve through royalties, adverting fees, distribution rights, or licensing rights. How they would earn a living, while helping others, was important but not paramount to seeing the first farm built. The celebrities themselves did not need the money, but the machine that got them to their celebrity status still needed regularly feeding.

Finding money was the job of agents who would negotiate that stuff with producers and sponsors. The agents were told to get the job done and do not kill the deal.

As for Stone, he wanted to open a new market for his environmental services and anaerobic digesters offered through WATER AIR SANITIATION AND POWER—WASP Environmental Design: but in the big picture, they would be only a small portion of the project until the building began; when water conservation, sanitation, and water pollution issues came to the forefront.

It was the pleasure of planting a seed and watching it take root and grow that everyone wanted to experience: to be part of something more meaningful than they ever had witnessed before: to live with purpose, to die with intent.

Stone was intimate with the darker side of humanity and knew the depths they could go destroying their own kind. Over the years, he had developed a basic understanding of the complex layers of events that caused his country and others to act the way they do towards the poorer less developed ones. Now perceptions and methods of the past had to change; everyone must benefit from the newest technologies and the lessons from the past, indemnify a sustainable future for the entire planet. His goal was to be part of an effort that called on humanity's higher nature. The work made for inspired dreams at night; the work paved a meaningful pathway for walking the Earth, when the morning came. Life on the blue-speck began to demand more from its occupants; more than breathing air and taking up space.

Stone was the lone nut on a hillside that began throwing ideas around. He was willing to shamelessly rip off his shirt and dance around until a few spectators thought it looked fun and began to join in. A movement was beginning, and soon Stone would blend into a sea of followers, each following the other followers: there was enough work for everyone—and it was all good. This was a sustainable feedback-loop. This type of feedback-loop caused the Universe to grow into its current ineffable complexity. Stone knew he was not floating in life's torrent by himself; he shares it with the history of thousands of others starting to converge on one destiny they were born to fulfill: a destiny, preordained millions of years ago, was beginning to emerge. Humanities brightness may be subdued under a basket by a selfish few, but eventually the light will burn through.

As the group moved from village to village, they would stop to collect surface soil and water samples. They also took GPS readings at soil boring sites, as they examined the substrates beneath the surface. Stone wanted to locate and characterize the ground and surface waters, while also measuring the topography of the land. Back home, he had organized a group of graduate students and engineering professors who had years of professional design and construction management experience. They offered to take the raw data and begin the conceptual layouts that would latter lead to the formal site-planning phase.

The group stopped at another tavern where they agreed to meet someone else. Unexpectedly they met an elderly farmer there. Pattie was an older man very close to ninety-five years old, a great achievement for anyone in this world but close to a miracle in Haiti. Pattie's face had deep weatherworn wrinkles; it rested on a body, held up by a frame comprised of thin sticks. He had crafty looking eyes that at the same time seemed sad and drawn. Nevertheless, those eyes, when you looked deeply into them, revealed an inner brightness that held almost a century of wisdom and a willingness to continue learning for another. Pattie expressed a profound concern for people that would come to his country with all the good intentions of helping, but not giving a thought as to the consequences. Everyone leaned forward and listened with interest. Bill asked him to explain.

By this time, Maurice had finished his other meeting and caught up with the group. Again, Maurice was visibly taken-back, as he was introduced to Bill Smith.

During the interruption, Pattie took a sip of sun tea and swirled it around his few remaining teeth, the way a pitcher would wind up his arm, as he got ready for a pitch. "In 1940, Ft. Liberte' was a fairly busy place," he began again. "There was a lot of activity. You see, the area around the bay was where we grew hemp and sisal for fibers. The United States Navy purchased all the rope and canvas the town could make from the harvest. All this activity required a lot of food for the workers. We had to grow it or catch it from the sea; there was no other way because all the markets were so far away. Consequently, a large fishing fleet started to build up in the port. We had a lot of Pelicans back then living around the bay and nesting on the islands.

"When the fishing fleet would come in with their catch, they would gut and head the fish, then throw the offal out to all the pelicans that were waiting behind the boats, or by the docks. These handouts were plentiful and so regular that the pelicans became lazy and therefore would never bother to go out and fish by themselves. During the day, while the boats were out fishing, the Pelicans just hung around the trees or floated in the bay. When the boats came in, they would eat.

"So, for at least 30 years these birds relied on the handouts given by the fishing fleet until one day the fleet disappeared. They had moved because the Navy stopped buying the rope. The war was over. Scientists also invented new methods to manufacture synthetic rope, from oil, cheaper. People lost their jobs and could no longer afford to buy the seafood. As prices went down to match demand, the fleet was abandoned because the fishermen could not afford fuel. Over the boom years, the older generations of pelicans that had traditionally showed their offspring how to fish had died off. Their parents taught none of the new pelicans how to dive for fish, so they began to starve and die. Soon all the pelicans died, and that is why today so few are seen here. I am afraid all of us in Haiti will soon die if we do not remember how to work and make our livelihoods from the sea and the soil once again, our nation must stop looking to others for handouts."

In his own folksy way, Patty had described a multi-variant positive feed back loop that drove his once thriving village into a state of hopelessness and despair. This wise man also knew how to reverse the loop, but until now, he had felt powerless to effect change. The group of followers was here to help men like Patty. They could only offer inspiration and resources, villagers such as Patty would have to do the work.

Everyone nodded his or her head in understanding as Bill roared; "Now that's what I'm talking about. No fooling, I am so part of this effort."

The goals of the 9 Tomato Program were once again outlined, and how they would be implemented. Meanwhile, Pattie listened with skepticism, an artifact of his years listening to empty promises. He also watched for any wavering from the truth. When the group was finished, Pattie nodded, and persisted with a wait-and-see posture.

    After interviewing a good cross-section of the various villages, Stone and the group, once again, set out to walk the land where they felt the farm had the best chance of success. It had good soil, and it was next to the mountains. There was plenty of water. No one lived on the land. Furthermore, Maurice's planned city would provide a market for the excess crops. It was also close enough for tourists to bike, walk, or rent a golf cart in order to visit the farm and the surrounding villages. All of the vegetation was secondary growth; there were no old growth forests. Nowhere in sight, was there a tree more than ten to fifteen years old. There was a good potential for wind generators on the cropland and pastures. There was a sparsely vegetated valley between two high ridges carved out by floods. This offered an opportunity to site a reservoir for a hydroelectric plant that could recharge during the day and overflow at night, generating electric power when there was no wind or sun: and provide much needed water for crop irrigation.

    The electricity would be essential to expanding the farm and the factories that would increase profit margins by adding value to the commodities. It would take a mixture of sustainable power sources to make it happen: wind, solar, biodigesters, and hydropower. Surplus electricity would subsidize power to the new sustainable city towards which Maurice had been working.

    Industry and tourism would eventually pay the bulk of the electric costs; the coop would pay a reduced but fair share. Electricity priced high enough that everyone would want to conserve power use.

    With this information on hand, it was time to get the support of the Haitian government. Bill eventually admitted the others sent him to observe and evaluate. After the meetings with the villagers and walking the proposed project site, and then learning more about the vision for the Ft. Liberte' area; once again, he declared his wagon was hitched to the program. He could not speak for the others but he had finalized his commitment.

TJ, filled with pride and sense of purpose, second only to when his children were born, was content. TJ was getting his 'mojo' back after a few years of crippling bad choices; a spin-off of too much success and too much money without the guidance and wisdom that comes with age. All great men, even presidents, have fallen to their vices: it is what they do to recover that history remembers.

TJ offered to fly everyone to Port-au-Prince for the next big meeting; however, Bill wanted to see the countryside so everyone agreed to drive together. After two hours of enduring bumpy rock roads, TJ was calling for the helicopter but could not get reception for his cell phone. Stone was bouncing up and down with Janet next to him. All the time he was thinking, she was going to be a lot of trouble for someone.

10

The Prime Minister

The truest nature of a Politian's humanity is unveiled when the fabric of their authority is ripped away; yet they continue to lead and inspire by example.

After a six-hour car trip south, driving along a rocky winding mountain road, the group arrived at their next destination. Brad Kitt, George Rooney, Forrest Whittier, Sean Glenn, and Matt Ramon all flew into Port-au-Prince to meet with Stone, TJ, Bill, and the Prime Minister Jean-Luc Bellevue. Stone would give the presentation. The others were there to show their support and to confirm their involvement personally to the Prime Minister. No one could imagine, just four months ago, the groundswell of support that was beginning to build.

The Prime Minister had also invited the Ministers of the Environment, Agriculture, and the Interior who also brought their assistants. The Ministers allowed their daughters and sons to come so they could ask for the celebrities' autographs. After the children were satisfied, they rushed out of the room allowing Stone to start the same presentation the others had received.

It was immediately obvious to the visitors how underappreciated these public servants were. The fact that their entire country was under siege was an understatement. There was no income, and there were no taxes to drive the government. Members of Parliament were missing or dead, or had deserted their posts. Police were trying to keep order and were working without pay. These were public servants truly working in the service of their community. These were the seeds of a new Haiti.

Over 1.5 million people were homeless. Eighty percent of the population was jobless, a statistic that the earthquake had not changed appreciably. Some government officials were under suspicion of taking bribes. At the docks and airport, it was a chaotic situation. The black market was flooded with donated food sold illegally. Loads of supplies and equipment were being detained until gangs masquerading as customs officials were paid the "import and state taxes" on the products. Friends like Tom Fuller, working for the U.S. Department of Transportation and U.S. Aid, helped Stone frame the issues facing Haiti. Everyone was trying to do what they could, in the worse constraints facing any nation.

The current President canceled the upcoming elections, which further delaying reconstruction for a year. A broken government was in place, but many conscientious employees had stepped up and continued to do their duty, even without pay. There was a desire to get things done, but done right. Hasty action could make things worse resulting in more disasters. This was a time to implement vision, and to use the help offered by the international community: an opportunity to rebuild structures and a thriving new sustainable economy. Bellevue was looking for a program that could bring action.

The problem was that expectations were high in the population that government would help to get them back in homes. Haiti has learned to live with dejection and anguish. Now they have been hearing and reading about hope. It is when hope is given, but not backed-up with action that dissidents become activated. The promise of hope would have to turn to action very quickly.

After the presentation, the Minister of the Environment wanted to hear about water resource protection. Stone showed him sketches of a proposed farm layout, mostly how digesters handled sanitation and provided water recovery opportunities. He talked about how the treated gray water would flush toilets. Additionally, how purified grey water would wash clothes and then supplement fishponds. Manmade-forested wetlands and vegetated wetlands would clean most of the water. The harvested fish provided protein for homeowners, and livestock.

The Minister of the Interior wanted to know what was in it for the government. Stone replied jobs, food, homes, and stability for the people. All the things the government could not afford to provide.

This was a chance for the government to step up. To claim responsibility for a program that would move Haiti into the twenty-first century and out of being the poorest nation on Earth. All it would cost them would be land that in any case, was not making the government revenues: To allow the farmers to live and work tax-free until their loans are repaid: to tax only those consumables not required to operate the farm or feed their families. The government would realize taxes when the products created by the farm sold to consumers: there would be a national consumer tax.

This was a chance for a new nation to avoid the pitfalls of big government. America is on the verge of financial collapse, as is Greece, Italy, Ireland, and a few other countries; all because governments are trying to be the answer to all the people's needs, instead of being a facilitator of opportunity and equality. Helping to establish farm cooperatives takes the responsibility of education, safety, medical, and food security off the shoulders of government, and puts those duties squarely upon each member of the cooperative.

Over 800,000 people would eventually have homes and own portions of their own businesses. Twenty cooperatives spread from north to south and connected by a great interstate highway would revive the Haitian economy and once again begin to generate revenue for the state.

The cooperatives would not be a burden. They would have their own schools and their own police forces with their own operating rules and laws. In times of emergency, the farm's police force could become part of a national guard, eliminating the need for an army. The police would have to report every quarter for training at a National Guard outpost.

Stone told the ministers that the cooperatives would become an important voting bloc that they themselves would help to create. The spillover from these farms would be educated voters and workers that would be paying taxes and helping the economy to grow.

There were no other plans on the table. Stone closed with a profound thought, "Hope followed by inaction is the birthplace of terror."

The Ministers looked at each other. Seeing consensus, they told the group they would support the program and call an emergency meeting of Parliament to obtain a formal agreement.

Before leaving, Prime Minister Bellevue took Stone by the arm and asked him to have tea at a nearby café. The others went ahead to their next destination. The "café" turned out to be some plywood nailed together with plastic over it. There were plywood tables out front with rickety chairs. The owners lived in the back and slept on the floor. To say it was a café was very polite and the owners seemed visibly honored to have the Prime Minister bring visitors to their place of business. It was Bellevue's attempt at community normalization in the wake of a storm. Knowing they had none to offer, Bellevue took out bottles of water and some tea bags from his backpack and handed them to the waiting "maître d'." The owners brought some water to a boil using remnants of the disaster. It was a surreal setting.

Bellevue stated the future had to start somewhere, if you believed there was a café in this spot then one day there would be. Today Bellevue insisted, by his example, this spot had a café and the owners believed they were the proprietors.

With the tea served, Bellevue tried to pay the owners who refused to take the money, but did when the Prime Minister insisted. Stone watched in appreciation.

"Mr. Richards, I fear Haiti is headed for even more disaster, not only from the rains that will soon come, but also from men outside this country that want to change our form of democracy, which is still very much in its infancy. Unregistered weapons are everywhere, with more smuggled in by the day. Further, I know training camps are being set up here and offshore established to train a secret rebel army, intend on taking control when the time is right.

"I love this land and its people," the Prime Minister concluded. "I have a vision of what Haiti can become."

Just then, two small children, a brother and sister both less than four years old, walked up with a little dandelion whose flower had just gone to seed; they handed it to the Prime Minister. He took it and blew on the seeds, setting them loose into the warm Caribbean breeze, free to find their new homes in the Haitian soil; a place where the seeds could grow their own roots and make their own new dandelion patches. He smiled while watching Stone, "Hope is a lot like that, isn't it Mr. Stone?"

"Indeed it is Mr. Prime Minister."

Bellevue had given these children food before, during his afternoon walks. He picked both up, and put them on his knees. He handed them some Madelaines the owners served with the tea; no doubt, looted from one of the imploded stores. He pulled from his backpack more bottled water and food bars to give the children.

"I am convinced, nonetheless" Bellevue continued, "that the 9 Tomato program has a chance to work and if successful could reshape Haiti for the better, something I have been working towards all my life. It is an experiment worth working on. I see where the vision could take us all. Here is my personal phone number. Call me if you need me. Anything you need my office will provide.

"The elections have been delayed and there is much turmoil. No one knows what the outcome will be. There are professional politicians and some entertainers with no business or government experience, all of them running for office at the same time.

"One entertainer responded, after being criticized for not having any political experience, 'How could I possibly do any worse?' Imagine the condition of a country where such a response is seriously considered.

"Some of those running for office will pay gangs to cause trouble and then blame that trouble on their opponents. In America, politics is a contact sport. In Haiti, it can be deadly.

"It is best you maintain your bottom up approach as much as possible, also with as little help from the government as possible. Even with our approval at the top, it is difficult to say how that will translate to the other influences. I can predict as you begin to show progress, a momentum will start that will be impossible to stop. Until that time, there will be some resistance before the momentum takes hold. What will you do when that happens?

Stone shrugged his shoulders while biting his lips a little, "Any recommendations?"

There was no immediate response.

After a few more minutes of details, the children were put back on their feet, both men stood up to shake hands. Stone nodded towards the Prime Ministers lap, which was soaked from two pairs of wet underpants. The media happened to be there with cameras watching the preoccupied man feed the children, and capturing a potentially embarrassing moment.

The Prime Minister looked down, and then smiled at Stone. Unflinching and oblivious to the cameras he said, "This is not new; it balances generosity: if you give something that doesn't require a concession back, many times you get soaked for it; I see this as a gift: a reminder if you will.

"Like the rest of Haiti these children need training and patience. Haiti has not seen unfettered opportunity for a long time. However, that does not mean they are not hungry for it. These wet marks serve to remind me to stay humble and reinforce my efforts to fulfill my purpose: yes, Mr. Richards, if there is no action soon, all of Haiti will be soaked. There are too many gifts not earned."

Unfortunately, of course, the media captured only the wet pants and left unrecorded the Prime Minister's metaphorical interpretation.

While Stone was attending the school of Bellevue, the celebrities had gone to Sean Glenn's tent city that he had been managing for more time than he cared to remember. They wanted to meet some of the residents: they wanted to understand more about the challenges they would face in selecting only 10,000 families out of millions that would become part of this great experiment.

Stone had wished they could have been part of this encounter with Bellevue. The force and the undercurrent that infused this leader's humanity was untold by the politics he had to endure to stay in power and keep Haiti together.

Glenn had a leg up on the others. He was on the ground and helping within 5 days of the disaster. Glenn may appear to be the bad boy of Hollywood, but his drive was to help those that others would deliberately try to hold down.

There was a depth and determination in Glenn unmatched in the others. Glenn was about action, not words.

There to greet them with a bodacious smile was the 'Prince of the Streets,' Jacques. Accompanying him was a Haitian entertainer named Mickey who was helping to hand out food and water. TJ thought there was something interesting about Mickey but could not find the words that described this affable character with a happy smile and a strong handshake.

Jacques grabbed Bill, TJ, Kitt, and Glenn dragging them from tent to tent introducing them as his very best friends to the rest of the community. Mickey, Matt, and Rooney held back continuing to pass out food and water.

Ben did not arrive in time to attend the meeting but jumped in to help the others distribute aid. Over the next 12 months, Ben would play a role nobody could foretell. Ben's role would leave an impression for generations to come, but not from the reality show.

After everyone acclimated to the hardships the residents had to endure daily, they boarded a plane destined for home to prepare for a very daunting next few months.

Stone had more meetings to attend and some challenges he hoped he would not have to face, but in advance, he would be prepared to exploit.

Sunny and his crew had been staying behind the scenes filming what they could; being a fly on the wall. Sunny and his crew had not been formally hired, but continued to work. They had gathered enough footage at this point to edit two documentaries.

Sunny knew there were two types of viewers he would have to satisfy. The first wanted action and drama the other wants details. His challenge was to satisfy the appetites of both. To accomplish that he would have to obtain funding for running two programs simultaneously, the first would be live action, and drama aired on the network, the other would be live meetings concerning engineering challenges and product development viewed on a web hosted design channel. Viewers, who had ideas that would help the engineers, could email suggestions. If viewers missed any of the events happening on either channel they could watch them again from the website as archived videos.

11

Michelin Louise-Perrier

Many times forceful elegance will trump a speeding bullet, but usually not.

Michelin Louise-Perrier was Haiti's Prime Minister before Bellevue. She left office in the midst of a flurry of corruption allegations generated by opposing members of Parliament. It was well known and accepted, she had been set-up, and the allegations were blatant lies: manufactured because she had gained great influence and support from the poorest of Haiti's people, who constituted over 80% of the population and thus 80% of the vote.

Any leader who effectively rallied the hopes and aspirations of the poor, in any country where the northern economies feared they were losing control of that nation's resources faced the same fate. The same lies were levied against President Aristide, which resulted in his exile, and against the Congo's Prime Minister Patrice Lumumba whose assassination was—admittedly--orchestrated by the American and Belgian secret services.

The President of Haiti, at the time, and his American "advisors," were concerned that if left unchecked, Louise-Perrier would take over power sooner than later—then they would be exactly where Aristide had taken them before. Michelin knew the dark side of Haitian politics and was an important asset for the success of the 9 Tomatoes a Day program. She had seen the books. She knew where to dig up bodies.

"Nice to meet you Mr. Stone Richards, how did your meeting go in the den of sharks?" Stone looked over this charming grandmother with a loving face and sweet sounding Caribbean voice, knowing that her tongue, backed by her bright and witty intellect, could very easily slice him to pieces.

"It could not have gone better," replied Stone. "Bellevue and his ministers were a great help. I am astonished by their commitment and by the depth of Bellevue. I was taken back, because I expected something completely different: mainly because of his involvement in your expulsion."

"Yes, I understand," she replied, "America is not the only country capable of subterfuge. Some have learned from our mistakes. When anyone in government displeases our benefactors, they are replaced and then obligingly, the new official talks the game corporations want to hear, while the others continue to do what is right. We do this and continue to work towards the same goal we have been seeking since Baby Doc lost power: freedom to use our resources to modernize our nation as we see fit. That goal, however, is consistently subverted by a few powerful and well placed turncoats, whose only concern is to line their pockets."

"I am on my way back north to finalize surveys and to stake out property boundaries that Bellevue has asked me to provide. By now, my boat should be there with some help," Stone reported.

The former Prime Minister stood up and walked into the garden, motioning for Stone to follow. "Bugs are everywhere these days and just not on the flowers. Bellevue is a very dedicated public servant and has been so for many years. He has a strong and hopeful vision for Haiti, but he needs much more support than he has. Some of his staff has rejected my help. He is afraid my presence could be a distraction.

"Mr. Stone Richards, you have a very ambitious plan. I like it very much. But do you have any idea how much a very powerful group of people do *not* like it?"

Stone took a seat on a bench next to the water fountain. "I know that anytime you do something different that threatens the status quo, fear becomes a bed partner for those who think they will lose the most."

"That is correct," said Madame Louise-Perrier, "and it is the landowners that will lose the most. For years, they have been able to use freely all the government's land without paying anything. If anyone farmed the land, the ones "managing" it had to be paid. Those in control here use intimidation and fear like the mafia of Palermo to control the population and make their money. You intend to change all that. Hell man, you do not even live in this country. A well-placed bullet could end all these fears."

Stone had already thought of that and plan B was dropping anchor in the shallows of Liberte' Bay at just that moment. "Madame, I hope I am not naïve enough to think that this effort will be without its detractors. But I am trying to invoke the higher nature of mankind with the support of a group of highly visible partners in an effort to land, not on the lower nature of mankind, but to achieve a middle ground somewhere in between."

"It will get very nasty, very quickly, Mr. Richards, perhaps more quickly than you think," mused Madame Louise-Perrier. "If you get in trouble, it is unlikely you will find favor from the courts or the government. Our Haitian Mafioso owns and controls the police, the prosecutors, and the judges: they are one, and the same. There are a few honorable men, but in order to survive they must stay behind the scenes until change begins to evolve."

Stone stood up and moved closer to the Prime Minister. "I am aware of these things and have walked in the shadows before. I just want to know, when it is time to voice your support and there is a call for your energy, can the program depend on you?"

The former Prime Minister came closer to Stone and held out her hand. "Mr. Stone Richards, your program will have my full support and that of those I try to represent."

12

Pulling Weeds

It is best to keep your friends close and your enemies tucked far away and out of sight.

It was raining when Stone pulled up to a dimly lit café in the old scenic town of Ft. Liberte'. The town had the feel and architecture of the French Quarters in New Orleans, but very much more run down. Sitting under a tarp was Buck drinking a beer. No one ever found out if he had a last name, or even a first; Stone never prodded.

The last time Buck had seen Stone was in Chania a few years after that time on the Turkey-Iraq border close to Lake Van. Buck had since "informally" retired as a Navy Seal team commander. He became a contractor who remained on call. They both stayed in contact by email and when Stone told Buck what he was up to, Buck jumped on the first plane to Florida and started to work. There were no questions asked. Buck and Stone both knew they could count on each other; that fact had been field-tested.

This time Buck had brought the *Spiritus*, Stone's fifty-four foot Jeanneau sailing yacht loaded with survey equipment, food, supplies, and a goodly arsenal of weapons and ammunition, just in case they might be needed. Buck's motto was "Don't ask for trouble, but be prepared to ship it back postage paid." Tom Fuller came up from Port-a-Prince to help divert customs from boarding the vessel. Buck and Tom had dealings with each other in the past. Neither asked questions of the other. Tom's dealings with U.S. Aid and the USDOT were sketchy, as were those provided by Buck and Stone. Tom had just left, returning to his base, but not until he and Buck had finished off a few bottles of wine and smoked a few contraband cigars, for old time's sake.

Buck tossed back a whiskey and stood up to face Stone saying, "Looks serious mate." Stone slapped him on the back, "Buck, let's get to the boat. Tomorrow is shaping up to be an exciting day."

Stone sat down in the cockpit of the *Spiritus* still wet from the first refreshing shower he had in a week. This was his fortress of tranquility and insight. *Spiritus,* in Latin, means 'divine inspiration.' Many times when inspiration was called for, it came to him just before the moments of waking; inspiration now comes to Stone carried by the winds blowing through this boats rigging.

Stone had managed through his life experiences to cull from his beliefs the religious dogma imposed on him during his younger, church-going years. He replaced it with a knowing that if there were a higher power, or a voice that life could tap into, it had evolved like all other manner of things, because of trial and error: it was his Librarian.

In his mind, religious dogma had no relevance to any natural force that had to evolve the same way in which all things did: religion was strictly a human thing; it had nothing to do with nature. This unseen and as yet immeasurable force whispered inspiration and drove purpose that added complexity to achieve the Universe's ultimate goal, which he imagined was, *do not waste the energy, lessons, and memory that has gotten life this far.*

Unlike religion, this natural force did not judge, execute, or demand; it had no other goal than to exist and accept humanity in the hopes that its highest potential evolved. That day would come when humanity finally finds a common purpose and strives to work towards it.

When he needed to clear his head and recharge, Stone would look to the *Spiritus* for help. He would yearn for the moment just after the engines cut out and the winds filled the sails, the only sound being the waves against the hull; the destination somewhere forward.

Buck jumped below and returned with a box of Cuban cigars and an unopened bottle of dark rum, contraband acquired during an emergency stop in Havana.

Something Buck could not explain had happened to the engine, and he had to dock in Havana for a weekend to check it out. "Honestly," Buck swore, "I would never think of violating the embargo. It was an emergency." Apparently the years' worth of cigars and rum just appeared out of nowhere in the supply cabinet, most likely put there by young, beautiful Cuban girls who liked sailboats and Buck's American dollars. Weapons and documentation were also easier to obtain in that country of contradictions, if you had the proper government contacts—and Buck always did.

Every time Stone opened a box of Fidel's best, the smells of Cuba's romantic tobaccos whirled in his head creating images of blue skies, clear, green waters, and mountain gorges full of endemic flora. These fleeting seconds were what life was about for Stone: breathing in every fragrance and tagging each of them with memories past and bracing for memories yet fulfilled. Lighting up and puffing, Stone reminisced with Buck looking on.

"Buck, I have tried pretty hard to maintain a peaceful life since our old days. I have risen above my ego as much as any good-looking guy can, but sooner or later you can always count on idealism colliding head on with reality. Once again, we are walking into the breach of a cosmic big bang that promises to mix things up. I think camouflage and some jiggery-pokery will be required to influence the outcome."

Buck shook his head a little—obviously understanding, "What's up?"

"I am pretty sure that sooner or later we are going to meet with stiff resistance," Stone replied, "and all the good we want to accomplish here is going to come to a halt until someone draws a line in the sand. I am afraid we may have to turn the tides and use the same underhanded tricks our detractors would use against us if allowed to do so.

"This goes high up, and they have offshore help. To add to the problem, there are idealists who are helping to fund this effort: they will not want to see violence used to achieve the required peace. In fact, I frankly cringe at the idea of falling back into that trap. The question is how to achieve peace in a land without law, and in a place where the detractors are the same people that would keep the status quo."

"And those same lightweights who want to promote change peacefully, are getting shot dead or exiled to other countries," growled Buck.

"It's a duality Stone. There is the idealist who wants peace and thinks everyone should give up his guns and armament while that completely ignores the fact the world is plagued with psychopaths that have no scruples. They steal and kill just as they breathe and walk, just to gain money and power; it is their sex: reason is not in their vocabulary.

"Yet, in times of danger an idealist wants someone to jump between them and danger. Like sex, they don't want violence discussed in polite society; it is only appreciated under the covers.

"We are strange birds Stone. It seems we have a tight rope to walk here with little forgiveness. Few men can walk the path we choose and still maintain a sense of idealism and righteousness, while continuing to hand an enemy a bloody hand-full of their own ass."

Stone just shook his head, "Buck, maybe one day you and I will find a place where we can live in a world of idealists and loose our cynicism. Until then I have to find a way to silence these guys and not lose the program's high ground. If there is a way around violence, I have not seen one yet."

"Call in the United Nations, Stone, make them earn their money." Buck murmured.

Cuban rum rushed up Stone's nose as he tried to choke back a laugh. "I think you know better than that. When you have a town full of rustlers, crooked sheriffs, and judges, the only friend you have is your gun. I would rather deal with the fallout from 500 well placed bullets, than ten more years of stratagem on this island. The American taxpayer deserves a legitimate effort to fix the problems here, and the Haitians have endured enough interference from American corporations, to have a real shot at success."

"Like always, buddy, you point and I will shoot. No questions asked. Let the devil sort it out, I say. The way I figure it, you will worry about the morality of it enough for the both of us. Then write a paper on it."

In the morning, Stone and Buck loaded up the truck and headed to the field. Buck took his backpack and made for the high ground. Stone shouldered the GPS backpack and headed out, setting property stakes and collecting data for the final site plan.

An hour later, Stone saw a vehicle coming up the road throwing dust high in the morning sun. He called to Buck, who was already on point.

The doors of the beat-up pickup opened up, while the wheels were still moving forward. The truck stopped just short of rolling over Stone's feet. Out poured four Haitians dressed for trouble and the local police commandant was by their sides.

From his old days, Stone knew how to handle authority that existed for its own self-interest and was prepared to fall into his old ways. Nonetheless, it did not take long for Stone to realize that this story had already been written in ink. There were no negotiations, or bribes, that would change this outcome. Two Haitians walked behind him with bats and two stood in front with bats as well.

The commandant said, "You are trespassing. "

Stone took the backpack off his shoulders and held it in front of him, "What do you want?" he projected in a low forceful voice. "I am here working on behalf of the Prime Minister."

The commandant moved closer. "Mr. Richards, we want you to leave now, and do not come back; if you do not leave, it will go badly for you."

Stone moved one foot back to brace his stance and turned to the side to minimize the target his body made. "I suppose no matter what I offer or do, you have orders to stop me."

With a rock hard stare the commander replied, "That is correct. We don't want you ever returning."

The front bats started to move. Subsequently, Stone noticed the thug's shadows on the ground behind him, were raising their bats. Stone smiled and asked, "Fine. Are you going to make my decision easy for me?"

"What the hell are you talking about?" the visibly angry commandant asked.

"That is whether I should be the judge, jury, and executioner concerning your life, or whether I allow you to beat the crap out of me." Stone growled.

"We will make that decision for you," replied the commandant.

Two flat thuds broke the ensuing silence, and the two Haitians in the back fell to the ground. The backpack that Stone was holding tore apart as bullets exited from it and landed in the chest cavities of the two Haitians in front.

The commandant stood with his mouth open. "I don't think so commandant," Stone said, evenly. "I tend to be a bit of a control freak."

With that, Stone shot the commandant in his left knee-cap, then walked over and stepped on the wound as the commandant rolled on the ground and screamed.

"I will give you a few minutes to think about what just happened," Stone said, "Then we will have another chat." Stone then walked over to look inside the truck. He turned and waved for Buck to come down.

As Stone returned to stand over the commandant he asked, "Now, are you ready to tell me who wants me out of here?"

"Damn you!" screamed the commandant, "Everyone wants you gone. They don't want your help!" It was obvious the pain was clouding the commandant's judgment, which is what Stone wanted; but the officer was still resisting.

Stone pulled back the hammer on the gun and yelled, "Names! Who wants me dead?" Stone waited for the man rolling on the ground to come to grips with his pain, in the hope names would follow: the names did not come, and the other kneecap blew apart.

After a few moments, Buck leaned down, while cracking open a vial of smelling salts, and passed it under the unconscious commandant's nose, until he woke up with a scream. "Welcome back for more," Buck said pleasantly, as the commandant slowly revived. Then he turned and looked at Stone, "Okay, it looks like he's ready for more. While you busy yourself here, I will begin loading up." For effect, Buck let the commandant hear the rest, "Just like the old days Stone, you take away a bullies power and bitch slap him around a bit, they break like a twig."

Stone leaned down close to the commandant and said, "I do not know any card tricks, and I am sure you know all the interrogation ploys I use. So let us just be truthful with each other. Do not challenge my patience. If you want to live, tell me who sent you here, and I mean everyone."

"All the elite, the families that rule Haiti." cried the commandant. "They don't want things to change."

"*Names!*" Stone yelled, and the names came one at a time.

Afterwards, Stone leaned against the truck and began to reload his pistol. "Every garden has a potential for beautiful flowers," he said, philosophically, "and every garden is always under attack from weeds and pests. Some flowers have natural defenses against such threats, but the younger plants are always the most tender and vulnerable. They survive by luck or with the help of a gardener. Buck, I think it is time to pull a few weeds before we plant the crops."

Buck walked up, shaking his head. "Damn, Stone, you have such a pretty way of putting things. You know, I don't think I have ever seen you hit a man in the 30 years I have known you. There is no way anyone can call you a violent person."

Stone looked at Buck with a blank stare.

Buck threw up his hands, "Hey, I'm just *saying!*"

Stone replied, "It's just easier to shoot the bastards, that way you don't break a nail…"

Buck also mused, "A historian could research your entire life, just by mapping misplaced knee caps. You might want to mix it up a bit more."

The commandant yelled, "I told you everything; can you please help me now?"

"Sure...straight to hell," Stone replied. A final shot rang out, the commandant went limp, and Stone's guns went back into the backpack. "Keep your friends close and your enemies hidden away," he muttered.

Buck turned quickly. "I shouldn't be surprised but why the hell did you do that?"

Stone replied, "Buck, he is a man use to power and getting his own way. I had no doubt he would have gone back and had us arrested for murdering these clowns. We don't have time for games or the luxury of justice. It is a hundred to one chance we get the only judge not paid by the same families trying to kill us now. This land is without order. We are working without a net, and whatever we accomplish has to happen quickly and without witness. Otherwise, the detractors will use their advantage and we will soon be dead."

Stone then began working out in his head the details of the next few days, the results of which would determine the success or failure of the entire 9 Tomatoes program.

Bellevue's fears were confirmed. There were internal and external forces working to change the government and Stone now had a roadmap detailed with names. Enemies of enemies had joined sides to take advantage of a wounded Haiti. If action does not start soon, Stone knew, the impatience of the masses would rally into horror. There would be no future for Haiti. Only civil war and chaos would result, a perfect scenario to justify a totalitarian rule that would shield narcotics, guns, and laundered money from public scrutiny.

Buck and Stone picked up the bodies and put them in the truck. "Buck, hide them away, I have a few more weeds to pull." With that, Stone got into his truck and headed off for Port-au-Prince.

While driving, Stone was thinking, if these weeds are not removed immediately, the project will not only fail here, but the hope for success in other parts of the world would also evaporate. If Haiti could become self-sufficient, and a serious player in the international markets, then America, Canada, and France, among others, could turn their altruistic efforts starting more programs in other depressed areas. If this farm program fails in Haiti, it will be used as an excuse to keep the same type of aid rolling along that solves no problems, but actually keeps ruthless dictators in power.

Over the next week, important heads of state and wealthy landowners mysteriously began to disappear without leaving word for anyone. Ambassadors and embassy staff from other countries vanished, their bank accounts drained. The Jackals and wolves that were the source and power of the elite were diminishing, making it harder for them to rally support for resistance against the farm cooperatives.

Stone feared the disappearances would lead to a gangster image instead of the otherwise worthy, altruistic effort the 9 Tomatoes a Day program was trying to build. He could have detained the detractors who crossed the line and tried to stop their work, but then who would be their judges? What laws if any were broken? What laws existed that say it is wrong to pay low wages and overcharge for food and clean water? Who would keep the detractors in jail?

In a land without law, separate rooms are required to maintain a healthy distance between reality and idealism. Kept in a stealthy vault, would be Stone's mischievous deeds that would otherwise paint him as an unprincipled hoodlum: they would remain known only to him and the sleepless nights that surely would follow this price for momentum.

Within weeks, gun shipments halted and drug trafficking ground to a stop. The organization that would have stopped Haiti's forward progress had been broken and scattered.

For a hundred years, Haiti had suffered one coup d'état after another, changing dictators for a new crop of corrupt government officials each time. Spoiled, were the most recent efforts to take advantage of Haiti's frailty.

The people had never before had a voice. This time, they would; a voice spoken with a determined and focused purpose backed by a plan, measured with goals. Clearly and unequivocally, it could be heard.

Less and Less objections to the plan aired in public or private. Soon even at the highest levels of government and the inner circles of the benevolent elite a new vision for Haiti had begun to unfold. Honest Judges and would be leaders began to peak out from behind their curtains.

Madame Louise-Perrier smiled in her garden as she had afternoon tea with a group of orphans five to ten years old who lived down the street. Change was coming, and this time it looked like it would be coming to stay. "Don't you think it is a wonderful day children? Can't you just smell the happiness returning to the air?"

Bellevue also found it easier to talk with the international community about the future and gain their support. There were, however, many questions about missing diplomats and once influential family members: Bellevue, honestly, had no answers. With bank accounts drained, he suggested they follow the money.

The world had turned upside down in Haiti; crushed by idealism, reality was forced to change. Hope danced on the sheets that covered the unmentioned violence that paved the way for change.

The story broke in the newspaper that the government had a plan to set up new farming cooperatives that would become self-contained, sustainable cities. The news spread through the camps. The biggest question was who would be the first to relocate?

Hope, finally, is backed by action.

13

Hollywood Dreaming

Change without timing is a desert without dry.

It had been a long time since so much anticipation flooded the executive halls of this major studio: two book deals, a feature movie, and a reality show with legs, all with the backing of stars willing to throw their backs and souls into the program.

Purpose entertainment, a brand new genre, has entered the industry. The old categories of fiction, non-fiction, reality, and memoir could not do justice to this new mix of words, voice, and motion that left social and environmental improvements in its wake. A fresh new proposal in the form of a docufiction novella, about a farm cooperative funded by a reality television show, which lifted millions of people out of poverty and set the global economy on an upward and sustainable path, was floating around.

The concept used advertising dollars, programming, books, films, reality shows, and product placement to attack and resolve pressing global problems while audiences looked on and even became involved if they so desired. This could be Hollywood's answer for a global stimulus package.

The conference room was full. The door swung open, and in walked a stern-looking man. "Who the hell is writing a thriller fiction novella that is more non-fiction than fiction about making a non-fiction reality show that literally pulls thousands of homeless Haitians out of poverty, giving them pride of home and business ownership? And what is all this confusion about heroes? The heroes are not only in the storyline of the books, movies, and game shows, but are also the viewers in homes, bars, and businesses; all riveted to their television, texting donations in the form of votes and dollars to the celebrity who gets the most results for that episode's work performance. It will never work--this is a complete waste of my time! Why the hell, are all of you sitting here? Go get that deal!" Harry Roan yelled his command. He was MGM's most aggressive dealmaker.

Forty years earlier, while walking in a park, Adara described to his son, Harry, the horrors and depths of evils that is harbored in the souls of every man. "What causes these things to rise to the surface, who can say? But what I do know is that when you work hard and have risen to a point where your life and work can make a better life for another, you have an obligation to do so."

Harry asked, "Who do I have this obligation to, father?"

"The Stars! We all owe our existence to the stars. And it is our obligation to continue their story and to complete their plan. Humanity can only reach its highest potential if we work together. Therefore, if you have a decision to make one day, to spend money to make a profit, or to do good, do the good. If you want to do better, make a profit while doing good."

Harry's managers thought he was mad going after the deal he had chosen. Then again, their father was not Adara the Noble, the survivor who, at the command of his mother, lived to force change.

A deal was cut with the Studio for the rights to the 9 Tomatoes a Day programming, which included the funding for the engineering. Purchase orders began flowing from producers, which advanced the delivery of construction materials and equipment. They also retained Buck and Stone as 'safety' consultants.

A team of studio executives and international attorneys, were sent to Haiti to secure the land and development rights.

The film crews, directors, and producers, all hastily assembled: their mission is to capture the excitement, the mayhem, and the successes or failures of ten teams, generated on a daily basis: each one helping to coach and manage 1000 novice farmers. Each challenge would take a monumental effort.

Sunny and his crew got the funding they requested. Harry would have no one else; he admired bold initiative.

A few months ago, Sunny received his "pink slip" when the Ophra Winfrey show went off the air. That is when Sunny agreed to take on the challenge of producing and directing the new reality show. The challenge and personal rewards, other than the salary provided by the work, was something he could not turn away. Working with a team who was motivated by the thought their work could improve the lives of many was nothing new to Sunny.

An extraordinary task he was faced with required a scheme that allowed the reality show to be taped, but at the same time to collect footage that could be used in the movie and a documentary.

It would require no less than forty cameras on the ground. Specialty cameras mounted on balloons. Others flown on remotely operated airplanes. There would be mobile camera crews and interviewers that would chase developing stories, and the resulting drama. There would be no shortage of action or thrills to capture and edit.

The show's narrator and in some cases mediator would have to be quick witted, personable, and well versed in matters concerning construction; as well as the social structure of the Haitian society. David Fallon won the bid. He was an unknown and very talented actor with a graduate degree from Harvard in public affairs and foreign policy. He was quick with a quip, polite, and very engaged with the idea of helping to make the shows affect the world something history will talk about for a long time.

All the actors, film crews, and experienced Haitian farmers, also serving as interpreters, and the team leaders assembled so they could receive instructions and clarifications on the mission statement, the goals of the farming cooperative, and the success criteria for the winning team of the challenge.

Bill Smith took the stage to talk to his fellow contestants. "I have been to the top of the mountain, and I have pictures to prove it. No really guys, you are going to get a kick out of this."

Stone's role seemingly started to fade, as others stepped up to take ownership of the vision. Bill had the program down solid and had no problems relaying the goals:

- To prove a business model that eventually becomes self-funded and lifts millions of people out of poverty while spiriting upward the global economy.

- To be successful in helping to obtain cooperative funding.

- To be the first to have homes built and to take the harvest to market.

- To maintain a high level of optimism. To advance the knowledge of farming practices, and cooperative living within one's team of farmers.

- To maintain a high happiness quota within one's farm team.

- To be entertaining while getting one's teeth kicked in by unexpected challenges.

There was another rabbit pulled out of a hat when it was announced to the assembled participants that Ronald Stump was convinced to blend some of his episodes with a few of the 9 Tomato episodes. His executives' would help in branding some of the value-added products to manufacture on the farm. They would also help to obtain shelf space in the larger supermarket chains for those products.

The blending of episodes would create cross-viewership and bring to the attention of more people faster, there is a bottom up solution to poverty, and that multiple marketing channels and networks were participating in the efforts.

Another challenge for Stump's executives was to set up a market and sell the carbon credits that the farms would be accumulating. This would help to generate immediate cash flows for the farms.

Ronald Stump's program would become purpose-oriented and green for a few shows. Viewers would learn about something they had never heard of before, and political leaders would see in real time how **Cap and Trade** operates: businesses that generate more greenhouse gases than they are allowed may purchase carbon-sequestering credits to bring their companies back into compliance. This creates jobs as poverty slowly becomes outdated, while new green products enter and revive a crippled global economy, and subsequently greenhouse gases ebb.

As the executives go about their business of competing with each other, Haitians who showed promise would be allowed to tag along to learn business from experts while getting experience in sales.

So now, there were two reality game shows working together for a common purpose. Economists could only scratch their heads, while trying to predict the future economy.

New economic models would have to include the concept that people realize that it is in their self-interest to help prop up those who are less fortunate. The new thinking would be that generating opportunities that will allow the least among us to contribute to the economy helps everyone. Helping people get into business, or just to survive, is not charity; it is good business and good government.

Intellectuals would begin to muse over the concept of what the world would look like if the 500 billion dollars spent annually on war and war machines, were turned instead towards funding innovative ideas. Ideas for water and energy conservation, education, energy generation, energy-efficient transportation, new ways to grow crops, reducing the ill effects of poverty, and funding start-up businesses, all which have always formed the core of employment in any country. With the old breeding grounds of terrorism, turned into the new flourishing grounds of consumerism, what justification was there to fund the fears created by the old machinery? It is a fact; trading partners do not fight: it is bad for business. They must compromise, accommodate, and cooperate.

The film crews and challenge teams went about their business fired up. They had vision and purpose. No one knew exactly how it would all happen, only that it must. They were determined to be part of this landmark life experience. Pessimism was not applauded.

14

Beginning Interviews – The Network Channel

There is one reality concerning a problem, there is always a solution.

On my mark 3...2...1, "Hello this is David Fallon speaking to you from the studios of '9 Tomatoes a Day' in Burbank, California. Can you imagine how uncomfortable it would be to determine the fate of an individual's dream? Even if that dream was to simply wake up with a little clean water to drink, and have a little food to eat: more so, what if you had the power to give it to them...or not?

"Except for my buddy Simon Howell, few people could ever look another in the eye on live television while telling them, "You will not be going to the next level:" they will have to find another way to survive.

That is what you will be witnessing here today, life and death decisions.

"Imagine doing that to a grandmother with six grandkids for whom she is caring. An opportunity lost, because her children died in the earthquake, and she is the grandkids only living relative. She is too old to work her share of the farm, and too busy with the small kids to do anything else. Insofar as it is possible to do so, emotions cannot be part of the selection process.

"The 9 Tomatoes a Day program depends on able-bodied people who can help build their own homes, work their portion of the fields, or work in some aspect of the cooperative so that the entire project will be successful.

"There is more at stake here than just the individual farms. The credibility of the entire business model depends on the collective efforts of all the individuals. If the model fails to work here, and if it is not proven that the farmers can feasibly pay back their farm loans, hundreds of millions of other people will lose the opportunity to lift their own families out of poverty. No, the Grandmother with six children to nurture must apply to another program until her kids are old enough to work.

"Or is there another solution? 3200 miles away in northern Haiti, a group of our coaches have assembled to de-bate, what may become, an issue so divisive, a solution may never be found; let's listen in to Stone, Matt, Sean, Rooney, and Kitt as they debate."

"This won't stand," Matt, complained, "I have a grand-mother. I love my grandmother. I will not kick this old woman to the wolves. I won't be a part of it."

Matt was on a roll, and he was obviously not a Simon Howell.

"There has got to be another way," he insisted.

George Rooney spoke up and said, "What have we got here? Six kids and a grandmother; according to the news agencies, there are over 500,000 kids in Haiti without grand-mothers or parents of any kind. How do we address that?"

Stone answered, "The primary goal is to make 9 Toma-toes a Day a working model for everyone to expand on. That takes able bodies and strong minds. Saving all the kids and grandmothers is another challenge."

"I cannot stand by knowing that grandmothers and kids will die on the street or in the mud, and I could have helped," Matt declared, without his usual smile. "Why is that red light on? If that damn camera is on, I am going to slap the shit out of somebody. Turn that damn thing off and I mean now!"

Stone tried adding to the group perspective, "There are over 45 million people unemployed in the USA, many of them veterans, and many of their families are living in cars or in tents. In Africa, parents are leaving their children on the side of the road to die because they are too weak to carry them to food and water. We have to pick our fights, he declared. There are wars to be fought everywhere. The dice landed here on these coordinates. As this program proves successful it can expand to other areas."

"So, what is the answer?" Kitt chimed in. "I am also concerned with the Kids without parent's issue." Kitt was in New Orleans speaking to the group via internet video. He was not due in Haiti for another week.

"Perhaps another layer of challenge," Stone replied, "but one separated from the 9 Tomato funding; however, it might somehow be molded into the 9 Tomatoes a Day program."

Stone grabbed a marker and went to the white board, "Maybe close to the proposed schools, we set up an orphanage. The grandmothers will take care of their children but also other orphans. Funding from NGOs or non-profits will help to provide building materials and food and to pay for electric. The kids will become wards of the farming cooperative, and the farmers will have to help raise these kids by sharing food, clothing, family time, etc. Because the orphans will be going to the same schools as the farm kids, perhaps we might luck out and the families will blend over time. No, I do not mean the orphans will live in the family homes, but at least the orphans will be invited to the homes to play with their friends and receive the family imprinting we all need and want from mothers and fathers. However, this requires a greater time commitment than you guys have already promised. You need to get the word out and find the funding and building materials. My group can draw up the building plans."

Matt said, "I'm in."

It was not long before all ten coaches had stepped up to dedicate their time, staff, and resources.

Sean Glenn chimed in at the last moment to state the obvious, "Now all we have to do is find this mystical grand-mother with the six kids."

"Now that did not take long," said David to his television audience. "What an amazing settlement to a very complex, and very real human drama, there in Haiti. So now, you have it. If you are a not-for-profit or even an individual and you like this solution to help the orphans and elderly grandmothers, text your support in the form of a donation, or go to www.9TOMATOESADAY.com and tell us how you can help Matt and the others get the orphanage built."

After the tent flaps opened, the sea of people rushed forward in one massive push, causing the applicants at the front of the line to fall on top of the table. Applications were now being taken, the criteria for selection a closely guarded secret. At the end of the day, there were over three thousand applications. It would be a long process.

Sky-cam 1 was catching all the action from a bird's eye view. Interviewers on the ground are talking with hopefuls that if chosen would move from a tent city in Port-au-Prince, to a modern tent city in Ft. Liberte': a place where they will become part of a daunting effort now underway to build a new farm community called Hope.

Sean Glenn, who had been gearing up for this moment, took another approach. Each coach selected the people he or she felt met the criteria, and Glenn had his shortlist already made. Within three days, Sean had all his families signed up, and he was ready to ship them to their new home. With his, no nonsense approach, Sean Glenn got his job done and was now in the lead.

The cameras caught up with Sean as he was heading to his tent. A link up was made with David, "Sean congratulations, I have Tom Banks screaming in my other ear that you are not playing fair; that you had a head start: got anything to say about that?"

The camera zoomed into Sean framing his upper torso as he put a cigarette in his mouth to light it. He showed the camera a pack of Lucky Strikes.

"Damn things will kill you, but if you have to die of something, I chose to die from a horrible lung cancer."

"Bank's is right David. Five days after the earthquake, my boots were on the ground and I was helping to get food and water to people who needed it. I was sweating my 'beep' off, swatting mosquitoes, smoking wet Strikes, and sleeping on the ground in a tent. Yes, I had a head start."

"How did you make your selections? What qualifications were you primarily interested in?"

"Firstly, there is a list of qualifications, which remains secret. Then I used my experience over the last twelve months to select those families that had both parents and children who, without asking, would chip-in to help maintain the camp my organization helps to operate. These people would show up to cook, collect the garbage, clean the port-a-potties, and pick up trash that others would throw to the ground. Over the last months, I kept mental notes of who those people were and had no question they would be great community leaders for the new farm.

"Next I looked at single mothers who found innovative ways to help each other. For instance, I found a couple of different groups that would pool their efforts and resources together. They pooled their food, water, and clothing. Then during the day one woman would stay with the children while the others went out to find work, food, or water. At night, they all pitched in and made a social effort out of cooking and cleaning up their living areas.

"Finally, I knew of single women and men that instead of loafing around all day, would show up at the operations tent and ask for work that needed to be done -- all without pay. They just knew it would take a group effort to stay alive. No one had to tell them, they just knew.

"I may not be the sharpest tack in the shed, but to me, that is exactly what the farm cooperative is trying to get people to do. They were selected because they were already workers who knew how to distribute and share the burden of work. They knew how to share."

"Thanks Sean, great work. This is David Fallon from the 9 Tomatoes a Day studios in Burbank, California asking that if you like Sean's judgment, while making selections that could change everything for a few people's lives, please text your donations or go to www.9tomatoesaday.com and tell us how you want to help.

15

Cash Flow Trails – The Design Channel

The trick to financial modeling is to leave enough room to jump out of the way of the boulders falling from the sky.

David Fallon prepared for the next segment would now concentrate on the collection and distribution of funds for the farms.

"Hello everyone and good evening, as our coaches continue in Haiti, preparing to move thousands of families to their new living quarters in Ft. Liberte', here in Burbank we are going to help you understand the monumental task that is involved with finding the funds to build a farm cooperative like the one proposed by 9 Tomatoes a Day.

"This may sound dry compared to the life and death struggle taking place in Haiti, but the team thought it was important to let you know how your donations would be spent and how it also helps us to bring in other funds from international agencies.

"I have with me today on the video monitor all the way from Haiti, Stone Richards who helped to put together the concept for building the 9 Tomatoes a Day farm cooperatives, hello Stone."

"Hi David, good to be with you."

"What inspired you, to devise this scheme?"

"That is not a one line answer so hold on. At least for me, the earthquake revived awareness of Haiti's poverty and the type of slavery it creates. Additionally, there was the poor economic state of the world, reduced American exports, environmental disasters in the Gulf of Mexico, joblessness in America, combined with companies and governments all looking for a way out; these opportunities opened unique avenues for creative solutions that just might provide answers and results, not only for Haiti but also for our problems in America.

"It was simply a matter of raising the awareness that creating 3 billion new consumers out of the poor, is in every person's self interest: at least from an environmental and economic perspective. Proving that the first farm could be successful was going to be, and still is a monumental task. The program simply had to have the right people behind it.

"So Stone, how did you go about doing that?"

"In the course of developing revenue streams and economic models, other important considerations had to be known and studied. We determined that in America, as well as in other countries, farmers in general were in a downward spiral. As there became less supply, the demand continued to rise and so did the price of food. It was obvious that more farms were needed to provide more food security and price stabilization. But the reasons behind the initial downward spiral of farms had to be understood before going forward.

"Economic models in the 1970s focused on increasing profits and reducing effort on the theory that in doing so, life for the farmer would improve. That meant that farmers had to specialize. The unexpected result was that farmers were put in direct competition with other farmers.

"In other words, the farmer with the most working capital and land would win in the specialization game at the expense of other farming families whose resources were limited. Additionally, because water, air, and dirt were not commodities that would yield a profit, they were not included in the economic models.

"As specialization became the norm in agriculture, the age-old wisdom that diversity increases safety was ignored: the risk of crop failures became more real. Crop insurance increased as a result. Multiple farms began to fold. As a result, there was less competition, and the cost of food increased so that now a pound of tomatoes would cost as much as $4.00 USD.

"So those are the basic reasons for the farm failures we witnessed in America.

"The economic model for the farming cooperatives had many factors to consider: The global market price of commodities is just one. The conservation of water and the restoration of native plant habitats; the restructuring of soils long ago degraded by erosion and poor farm practices; and organic farming requirements are some others.

"Then there are the needs of other farmers out side our cooperatives in Haiti, the sustainable nature of everyone's farming practices, diversity of all the crops and livestock; all that would serve to increase harvest diversity and reduce risks. But most importantly, we wanted to consider the lifestyles and the happiness factors that impact the farmers and their families. The farmers needed to have a lifestyle that would allow them to work to live, and not just live to work. We wanted to build a community not just a farm.

"The families also needed to have access to healthcare and to know that their children had access to high quality education. Art, culture, and freedom of expression needed weaving into the community lifestyle.

"Factories that could add value to the harvest would help to increase profit, reduce market risks, increase the number of jobs, and help merge products into global markets. This was the core premise of the farming initiatives.

"With this information established as our foundation, a plan was developed that considered why the past failures happened. From that we began to pool as many ideas and resources together that we could, so that the funding we needed could be found.

"Seed capital must be organized so that basic farm requirements could be met and harvests realized. This money would come from a stream of revenues, services, products, and new, innovative ideas such as this reality show. In addition to the donations your viewers contribute, other sources of revenue help to build infrastructure and purchase the initial farm inputs. Such as these:

Stone created a brief list of opportunities targeted as high-level possibilities:

- NGOs (Non-Governmental Organizations) give start up food and water.

- USAID provides temporary Tents and Generators.

- USAID or the World Bank provides loans for roads, bio-digesters, and a hydro-powered electric plant.

- Building materials provided at discounted prices by vendors or national chains.

- Actors trade their time on the celebrity show for a stake in the movie profits.

- Maurice provides land for a resort near the beachfront to house the celebrities and their families.

- Universities donate time to train the farmers and help set up a best farming practices document.

- Supply contract agreements set up with Wal-Mart and Publix grocery stores.

- Money from donations collected on the website used to purchase used farming equipment, earth moving equipment, seed, livestock, pumps and irrigation piping, flat bed trucks, and fencing materials.

- Shipping of supplies and materials to be provided by the US Navy.

- Volunteers from all over the world would be invited to sign up as team members who work under the celebrities.

- The celebrity game show would receive money from each text sent in support of a certain celebrity for their well-done job.

- TV Stations worldwide offer free airtime for the celebrities to make their pitches to support their teams.

- TV Stations will pay fees to air the show.

- Sponsors could donate their products for use in the co-operative as a product placement opportunity, showing the world how their products solve problems.

- Sponsors will pay for the opportunity to demonstrate that they are concerned about more than profits; that they are participants in the changing view of how business and humanity interact on a global basis.

- Manufacturers will hire contractors and farm labor to build their factories. These buildings will house equipment whose purpose will add value to farm-raised products; products that sequester atmospheric carbon.

- The US Congress would lift trade restrictions, making it easier for Haiti to export to US markets.

- Purchase orders transferred from China to Haiti to take advantage of the cheaper labor and lower costs for shipping to the USA.

- Textile companies agree to locate in Haiti to take advantage of its Kenaf crop and the low labor costs.

- TJ Hoods will design a world-class golf course and sports complex on Maurice's land adjacent to an exclusive beach front resort that would be the home of the actors and film crews for the next twelve months.

- A boat yard would be opened on Maurice's land that would attract mega-yachts wanting to lay over for repairs, maintenance, or storage. This would provide other jobs for the farmers.

- USAID will provide funding for a new port that would also support an industrial park and docks for cruise ships, creating even more jobs.

- A five hundred-room beachfront resort would be built to house the celebrities and volunteers during the game show and movie filming. The ownership and operation would be turned over to the cooperative after production is completed. All proceeds to benefit the cooperative.

- Investors would finance beachfront and farm view bed and breakfast motels as 40/40/20 percent owners. The cooperative management team would provide sales and administrative assistance to the operators and help to insure the safety of the investment for 20%.

- Funds that come in for the orphans along with beds, furniture, computers, clothing, books, and something the kids have never heard of or seen before--pajamas. Now the kids would be able to take baths, put on their pajamas, and be read bedtime stories by their den mothers before they drift off to sleep, very different from sleeping with an empty stomach on a concrete floor wearing the same clothes week after week. All the celebrities would donate substantially to make this happen. The kids would grow up knowing that complete strangers cared about them, and that they were not alone in the world. They would also realize that they live in a community that mentors them and protects them so that they have the greatest chance of success and happiness in life.

"Wow, my head is spinning."

"I know David; there are a lot of opportunities to fund this farm. There is also a lot of information we want to make available for those who want to participate. Therefore, they can go to www.9TomatoesaDay.com to find more information and learn about other ways they can get involved.

"David, the only thing more important to us than building the farms, is making sure the people who help by donating are well informed as to how the money is used, and are able to see the real time progress as the farm springs from the ground.

"Thanks Stone, get out of that air conditioning and back in the field so those people can soon have their own food and shelter. Thanks for your efforts, Stone.

"Ok, from the air conditioned war room in Haiti, we now go to the construction trailer with TJ, Stone, and the engineers to hear them discuss the last minute details they are putting together before the big push begins."

16

Hope Begins – The Design Channel

New ideas succeed when the innovator is a bigger bastard than the traditionalist is, but mostly when money exchanges hands.

As heavy excavators began to turn the Haitian dirt and rock, 'New Hope' sprung to life. In just 10 months since its inception, the dream team of celebrities, experts, and business people had managed to move heaven and earth to make it happen. They did not do it alone, however, and they knew it; there were hundreds of other people working daily behind the scenes.

Roads, drainage ditches, multipurpose ponds, housing pads, and the multipurpose security rim ditch all had to be built, and the grounds seeded before ten thousand families could begin to show up. Permits had to be obtained, sponsors and investors satisfied, all while the logistics of moving millions of dollars of materials and equipment from Cape Canaveral, Florida to Ft. Liberte' seemed insurmountable; but there were those that made it look easy.

"We are back again, and I am your Host David Fallon. Assembled are the experts whose task it is, to make this farm community a reality. The farm's design takes into consideration soil conservation, water protection, crop and livestock diversity, comfort of field workers, farming efficiencies, native plant and animal protection, community culture, business, economic diversity and profit margins, just to name a few things of course.

"What I really like is this farm will employ alley farming practices. It is not only practical, economically speaking, but is essential for ecotourism. Alley farming plants rows of trees that will yield a harvest, be it food or wood, in between other annual or bi-annual crops. This allows the fields to look mani-cured, year round, even after they were freshly plowed. The trees also act as windbreaks helping to protect the crops and topsoil. Moreover, when there are no crops to harvest there would always be fruits, cocoa, berries, and nuts. The rows of planted trees also serve a dual purpose providing interesting hiking, horseback, or biking trails for adventurous tourists.

"I don't know about you, it seems like a wonderful place to visit, but I am thinking I would prefer to live there when all is said and done. Let's listen in."

TJ was offering a suggestion that tree lined fairways for a golf course, can also be incorporated between crops. "Look all you have to do is open up the alleys between the crops and I will slide a fairway in between. The Tee and the greens can be placed at the intersections of diverging fields."

Esteban, a farming engineer complained that the fields would be reduced in size and would not be practical to plant. TJ answered, "Then why don't you plant high value crops such as sunflower? It would help create more buzz to play the field when the flowers are in bloom and make a creative backdrop for the cafes and kiosks that will line the trails and walkways."

Of course, the first thing the engineers wanted to do was reengineer the work the other engineers had already done. Why you ask, because, that is what they do.

The first item up for discussion addressed the question, why are we building a farm. What the Haitians needed was housing. "Why don't we just build the houses and move on?" Someone asked.

Stone again went a little cross-eyed. With all the papers he wrote and the lectures he taped, there were still engineers who would not move out of their little box. Instead of snapping in front of the cameras, Stone put his best effort forward and tried to explain once more,

"People need a fully bell before they need a home, and even before that, they need to see a future. Otherwise, all you are doing is building them a coffin. Any community we build needs to take into consideration food, jobs, medical, sanitation, and then shelter. Everyone can live in a tent if they have to. They cannot eat a house. The farm is going to provide a diversity of food, jobs in agriculture, jobs in manufacturing, and service jobs. Every detail must be considered so that the farm community will be sustainable not only economically but also environmentally. It must be an economy that can maintain itself if it is isolated, or survive shocks if allowed to compete in the global economy. It must be designed under the principles of Economic Shock Buffer Design.

Allen was one of the older, more traditional engineers from Louisiana, "I just don't get why we gonna risk using a brand new technology for sanitation when we could build a sewer plant a lot cheaper." Stone asked, "How much cheaper?"

"We could build a sewer plant for $10,000 per home," Allen replied.

Stone set the hook: "Does that also include the sewer plant, or just the collection system? Does it also include cooking fuel for the homes and gas for transportation and electrical generation?"

"Well of course not," Allen rumbled, "The sewer plant is an additional $10 per gallon per day. I am very uncomfortable with you mixing apples and oranges; a sewer plant is designed to treat sewage. You don't mix uses by also designing to produce electricity."

"So that is $10,000 per home for the collection and transfer system plus another $2000 per home for the treatment plant," Stone summarized. "Yes," Allen replied.

"Ok," said Stone, "Do you have an engineering reason why a sewer plant cannot also provide gas for cooking, transportation, and electrical generation?

"Not without further study, no I don't." Allen replied testily. My point is made based on years of engineering design and project management."

Stone's rebuttal was pithy, "Anaerobic Digesters have been in use for over 500 years. The technology is not new. As microbes digest the organics in sewage, just like in a septic tank, or a traditional sewer plant, methane gas is produced. We collect that gas and use it for cooking, heating water, or running engines. Use of this "biogas" is the same as using natural gas. Both are products containing methane. All the modern electrical power plants in America are now using natural gas.

"There is still the constant upkeep, the maintenance and meticulous testing that a sewer system would have, but those costs are dramatically reduced further by spreading them over the multiple products they yield like electricity, gas, fertilizers, and irrigation water."

Stone then displayed a plumbing and flow diagram of a digester on the wall. "At a projected 2 million gallons of water per day, we are looking at 7 million US dollars for the digesters and electrical power equipment plus, 10 million US dollars for the collection system. Amortized over 15 years, for 10,000 homes with 5 persons per home, that is less than $0.062 cents USD per day for sanitation, gas, and electric per person. That is $0.31 per family or the cost of one tomato a day.

"You are not including all the facts," Allen protested. "A sewer plant can also clean up and return to the homes all the water reclaimed for the same uses."

"Great, but at what cost? And can traditional sewer plants produce electric and cooking fuels? Let's face it, a digester is nothing more than a closed system sewer plant that is able to produce useful by-products" Stone was about done with this part of the discussion.

Stone walked across the room to the white board, laid out the cost comparisons in two columns, and then asked Allen and the others, "Is there any disagreement that digesters are the more cost-effective choice?"

Because of the way the quadraplexes were laid out, the plumbing costs were under $300 per unit. Each dwelling also had its own toilet. The plumbing, electric, and gray water treatment were all shared. By now, the younger engineers had logged into Stone's website to review the specifications and to get more data:

www.waspenvironmentaldesign.com

"But these people are not accustomed to such technology," Allen droned.

"That may be so," Stone replied, "but they are also not accustomed to sewer plants. But just as sewer plants require trained technicians, there will be trained and certified technicians who will work for the cooperative's AD utility. All the homeowners have to do is flush the toilet. I think they can probably do that."

Reluctantly, Allen relented and grudgingly agreed that digesters were more suitable in this situation than a sewer plant would be. The other engineers also agreed, and the discussion shifted to other infrastructure demands.

Providing ports, electricity, and road infrastructure would become central to uniting Haiti and unleashing its economic potential. Northern Haiti provided the best location in which to start due to its strategic location, geomorphology, water, and the potential for a fresh start. A strategic move for rebuilding Port-au-Prince was too get as many people as possible out of the city and back into the country side. Farm cooperatives helped with that plan.

Two large wind generators would also be installed in the cooperative. These generators, powered by the Atlantic sea breezes, would provide enough electricity to power the farm, the manufacturing operations, and the homes in the evening.

Finally, as the farm becomes profitable and Maurice's new city is built, a hydro-powered electrical plant would be built in the foothills.

This first farming cooperative would generate enough electrical power to supply not only the farm and the industrial component, but also parts of the new oceanfront resort city, and Cape Haitian, located 20 miles to the south.

The existing road connecting Cape Haitian and Ft. Liberte' would be widened to four lanes, and it would represent the start of the backbone of Haiti's new transportation system.

"Hey guys, it's David Fallon, we have been spying on your meeting and I am just wondering. How does a guy like me get to live on the cooperative, and enjoy the great lifestyle, even if I do not want to work on it?"

Stone took the question, "David our plans are to build a few retirement communities outside of the cooperative. For instance, up on the mountainside next to the proposed water reservoir we will construct a Tuscan style community. You could buy or rent a place there and everyone is welcomed to enjoy the parks, landscapes, fresh organic food, and entertainment provided by the cooperative members. Additionally, as the seaside sustainable community develops--just a bike ride away--there will be homes and condominiums that will fall into a wide market range. Additionally, locals can purchase seasonal supply contracts for fresh dairy products and produce that can be delivered to their homes. The onsite Farmer's Market and Entertainment Center will always be open to the public."

"Stone seriously, count me in. I could not think of a better get away place. Thanks.

"And if the audience wants to learn more about living accommodations around New Hope, Haiti, or vacation packages just go to www.9TomatoesaDay.com to find out more.

"In our next show we will be learning a little about how the farm will be managed and who will be monitoring the spending of your contributions. Until then goodnight and God bless. I am David Fallon and this was living on just 9 Tomatoes a Day."

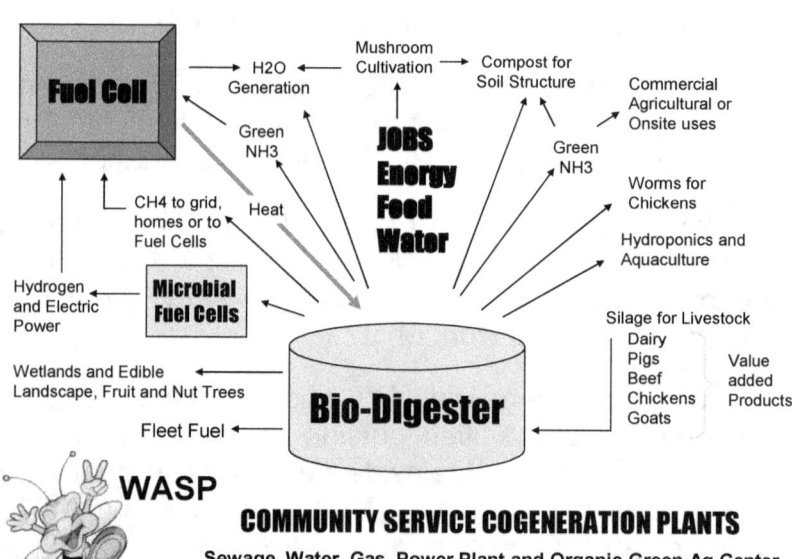

COMMUNITY SERVICE COGENERATION PLANTS
Sewage, Water, Gas, Power Plant and Organic Green Ag Center

17

Management Teams – The Network Channel

Highly skilled professionals are wanted, who will work for low wages and train their replacement.

Jean-Baptist is a Harvard graduate with a Juris Doctorate degree in law and has an MBA from the Rosen College of Hospitality Management. When he was twelve years old, his mother took him to live in Orlando, Florida with relatives that worked for a large resort motel.

Jean-Baptist was an avid reader while he was growing up. His mother did not have enough money to send him to the mission schools, so he took it upon himself to learn. He used his big smile and tenaciousness to wrangle the admiration and respect from one of the teachers at the school. The teacher would give Jean-Baptist just a few lessons then send him home with some exercises.

Jean always returned with the work fully completed and perfectly done. At night, Jean and his mother, who was also illiterate but wanted to learn, would sit at a small wooden table, with only a homemade candle to illuminate the pages, and he would teach her the lesson for the day that he received just hours before.

From pre-school readers, to comics, up to high school texts, Jean-Baptist excelled in reading and more so, he was able to piece together independent concepts into larger notable ideas. He was a natural: a diamond in the rough, as some would say. He so impressed his teacher with his competency, she convinced the school to grant him a full tuition wavier and to give him a uniform so that the other children would not make fun of his tattered street cloths.

When the doors of the school opened, Jean-Baptist was always there. He was on a mission. He was going to be a businessperson and one day build his mother a new house, and be able to buy enough food that she would never again have to go hungry, while he ate the last crumbs.

Harry Rosen is a self-made billionaire that worked his way up to the top--the hard way. He owned a number of resorts in the Orlando area and employed over 3000 Haitians that helped to keep his properties operating to the highest standards that he demanded.

One day a Haitian assistant was telling Harry about his nephew who received a grant by a mission school, and the reasons behind the achievements. Harry had always had a deep nagging sense of responsibility for people, events, and things that, even if he ignored them, would never otherwise affect his life. He just cared. He also knew that life for him could have gone completely in the other direction. If just one parameter were to have shifted in the slightest direction, left or right, many things would be different.

Harry began to ask questions about the boy. Over the next few days, he had an assistant call the mission school to learn about this wonder student. Eventually, he called the school himself and asked the attendant to find Jean-Baptist and put him on the phone. Jean-Baptist, who never before talked on a phone, answered: it took him a few minutes to figure out the contraption.

The voice at the other end was speaking in Creole, "Jean-Baptist I understand from your uncle that lives in Florida that you are 'li fo' anpil ti gasson' (a very smart boy), is that true?"

"I really do not know what smart is Msye. My teachers say I am 'yon etid rapid' (a quick study), but as far as I know I only do what I like to do, I like to read books and learn."

"Jean-Baptist what do you want to do with all this new knowledge?"

"I will become a great business man."

"And do what as a great business man?"

"I do not know that: but I am sure it will come to me just as when I am hungry, food appears."

"How is your English?"

"I speak and read English, French, and Creole very well thank you."

"I am very impressed. And you did this all by yourself?"

"No Myse, my teachers taught me. I just completed the exercises."

"Would you go home and talk with your mother and ask her if both of you can come to Florida and live with your uncle? Tell her, I will pay for the costs of travel and I will give her a job in my hotel; and you Myse, will attend schools here and if you are as smart as your teachers say, you can come to my college when you get out of high school…what do you think about that?"

"I have nothing to say Myse. It sounds too good."

"I suggest you go get your mother and have her ask the mission to dial my number for her to talk with me directly. They will do this I promise. I will talk with your mother and see if we can get you here to attend American schools and universities. I only ask that one day you return to Haiti and use your smartness to help other children just like yourself. Never forget how life is for you now, and how much better it could be. Ok?"

"Repons lan se wi mesye: yes sir."

"It was nice meeting with you Jean-Baptist; I look forward to meeting you in person. Now can you put your teacher back on the phone for me please?"

Jean-Baptist ran from the schoolhouse to retrieve his mother all the while thinking he really likes phones.

"On three, 1...2...3, hello this is David Fallon coming to you with the coaches of 9 Tomatoes a Day.

"Building a management team for the cooperatives can be a tricky process. People are needed who want to make the greatest impact while working themselves out of a job. It may take five to fifteen years to train everyone, but in the end, the Haitians will manage and operate their farm cooperative. The ultimate goal would be to find young people who live in the cooperatives, then train and school them in business management as they work up through the ranks. The Haitian farmers would be the owners, and it would be their business; the outsiders would be there to help keep the vision alive that gave the first farmers the initial opportunity.

"Today we are speaking with the CEO of the 'New Hope' farm cooperative Jean-Baptist. He grew up in a town called Thomonde. A benefactor brought Jean to America and paid for his education. Now Jean-Baptist is back in Haiti paying forward that kindness by helping to manage this epic effort to rebuild an entire nation from the bottom-up.

"Speaking to us via internet video from Ft. Liberte', Jean-Baptist are you there, can you hear us?"

"Yes, thank you David, it is a privilege to be talking with you and your audience."

"So Jean you are tasked with building the management team that will run the day to day operations of the farm. You have full profit and lost responsibilities, how is that going?"

"As you can imagine it is a massive challenge. If you do not mind I would like to have anyone who needs employment and has worked at an executive level in the past running farms, food processing plants, manufacturing operations, or managing sales and marketing efforts, please go to our website www.9TomatoesaDay.com and fill out an application. We are looking for the top experts in their field. Depending on the position, your time will be split between corporate offices located in Florida and here in Ft. Liberte'.

"As donors we are obviously concerned that the money is spent on building the farms and getting operations up and running. Who is monitoring the spending?"

"David we have a Board of Directors, who oversees the management team and the budget spending. They were chosen from a group of international donors who share the vision of 9 Tomatoes a Day. They are tasked with making sure that the money is spent in a manner that is appropriate to building the dream and keeping it alive.

"The Clinton Oversight Committee is also involved as an outside auditing group that helps to insure other donors that their funds are spent for the purposes intended and that there will be no corruption."

"Jean what other funds have you collected for the start up?"

"Currently we have corporate sponsors who have pledged a percentage of their gross sales to the 9 Tomatoes a Day program and have offered management assistance and technology training. The work and funds these corporations have provided has been irreplaceable. A dollar value is very difficult to attach to the achievements for which they are responsible."

"You have investors that showed up and are putting up manufacturing facilities. What protects their investment should the government change once again?"

"I can understand why you would ask such a question David. The government has passed laws that give clear title to the land for a business that builds a factory and hires Haitians. Insurance is also available that insures against failures in the government that would cause the loss of ownership. The international community and the World Bank will keep pressure on the Haitian government to keep and maintain their contracts and agreements.

"Even more interesting is that the government has given extraordinary powers to the farm communities to self govern and to provide their own security force. Even though the security force would become part of a national guard in times of emergency and answer to the President, their primary mission is to protect the sovereignty of the farm and protect its people and their investment. We have hired Haitians for this effort but also former French and American paramilitary trained soldiers who bring expertise and professionalism to the units."

"Jean, how do the owners get a say in how their farm is to be run?"

"They have representation in the Owner Advisory Board. It is comprised of 30 elected individuals consisting of three qualified persons elected from each POD containing 1000 families. This group ratifies the farming cooperative operating agreement. All owners will have to sign and agree to it before taking possession of their houses and their portions of the farm. It would be the responsibility of the Advisory Board Members to keep the families in their PODs informed and to represent a POD's concerns to the rest of the cooperative and to management. The contracts are simple, in exchange for work and cooperation, the cooperative uses its best efforts to provide housing, food, clothing, education, and medical services.

"The Owner Advisory Board elects an Arbitration Board. The Arbitration Board would settle disputes between owners, and between owners and the cooperative, and would enforce the intent of the operating agreement. You don't need a law degree here: you just need wisdom, patience, and a strong sense of justice."

"Jean it sounds like they have you covered top to bottom, like cheese on rice. Doesn't that make it hard for you to do your job?"

"Not at all David, my intent is to make this farm flourish so that more farms can be built that can serve more people. I leave the accounting to the accountants and I focus on how to add value to the crops the farmers produce, and getting them sold to the highest bidder. I manage costs and try to improve efficiencies."

"Jean we know about your history with education. What are you doing to promote education on the farms?"

"We have a Board of Education that is responsible for the hiring of schoolteachers and the training of children not only in farming practices but in the arts, math, reading, science, and technical skills.

"Because farm cooperatives are intended to link many nations; economics and foreign policy are to be taught heavily so that the pearls can be plucked from the crop as they evolve. The greatest deterrent against the abuse of power, in my opinion, is information, and training people how to use it.

"We have computers for each child and they teach themselves, at their own pace, using lessons found on the www.khanacademy.com website. The teachers are there to coach the students. The students learn to ask the right quest-ions then go find the answers for themselves. I think it is a re-markable program. We are seeing early success."

"How are you handling medical, Jean?

"We have built a very nice hospital for the doctors, their interns, and the nurse practitioners. We have a medical board comprised of volunteer doctors who rotate shifts on the island. We provide every convenience they require. The interns stay here full time, and the doctors rotate but are always available via internet video for a consultation. It will be difficult in the fu-ture to tell if they are here to help the people, play on the TJ HOOD golf courses, or catch trophy fish off the inlet."

"Isn't it nice that they can actually do all that if they choose to Jean? There is a lot of misery in that region and sometimes you just need a break. Jean, what about the Or-phanage, Matt and the others were quit concerned about that program being made a priority."

"The Orphanage falls into a unique position within the cooperative. The management team helps to keep the facility running and funded. Education will help to get the children prepared for their future lives. The families of the cooperative will take responsibility for mentoring the children and giving them a sense of community. Not-for-profits and private funding will keep the Orphanage operational. My mother, who now lives in Miami, comes here for months on end and helps to raise the kids. The older ones that show promise move to her home and attend university in Florida. It has become a very full house."

"That is amazing Jean; we know that the orphanage was an afterthought but what a testament to the flexibility of the founders and the others working on this program. Tell us how does the workers, the owners get reimbursement for their labor?"

"Blackberry and IBM CEO Bob Manner stepped up to turn his advertising machine towards purpose entertainment. Instead of paying for the creation of advertisements, Manner directed his marketing and product development people to work with our Owner Management division to design a program, and a card reader system that will help manage the database of work hours, harvests, and store expenditures of every farmer and family member. This effort represented a big cost. Nevertheless, it is paying off for IBM because hundreds of manufacturing companies, worldwide, are seeing the product in action on this show, then call IBM to find out more. For the cooperative, the ability to transmit work assignments, track job progress, and harvests made by the farmers, all from an identification card is invaluable."

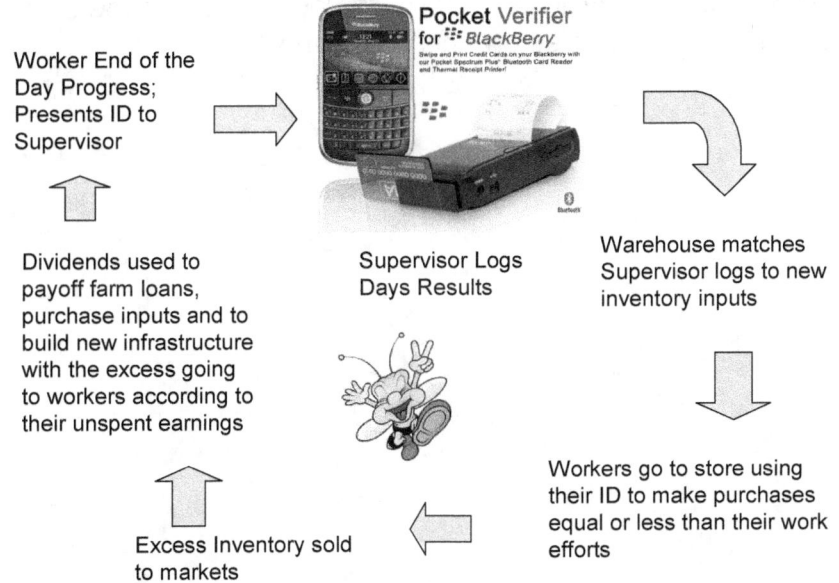

"One final question Jean, Why? You are a very prominent lawyer and CEO with a MBA. Why not go for the big bucks?"

"David, there is no amount of money that can equal the rewards I receive from doing this work. I am leading the charge of one of the biggest ideas since computers and the internet. This is the biggest war ever fought in history. When it is won, no war will ever have a bigger more positive impact on society. When we are successful here, the march continues to the Niger Delta, the Thai Burma border regions, the Congo, and the Horn of Africa; anywhere there is rampant poverty and our model can help.

"But in the end it is really because of a promise made years ago to a complete stranger who just as well, could have never got involved in my life. He made all the difference and there was no monetary reward for him. He just wanted to make a difference in a child's life. He only asked that I re-member where I came from and to help others when I can. I am keeping that promise. Harry if you can hear me; thanks many times over…mission accomplished."

18

Tent Cities and Bathhouses – The Network Channel

The problem with launching new products using social media is that all the warts are exposed as you pull your pants down.

The bathhouse and temporary housing plots were seeded with grass. Now it was time to build the bathhouses. The next step would be to ship in the residents.

The forms for the bathhouse foundations were in place, and the concrete was pouring. The bathhouses have ten low flush toilets, ten showers, and ten sinks for men in one-half and the same equipment for women in the other half.

As the permanent homes are built, the plumbing fixtures would be taken out of the bathhouses, refurbished, and put into the permanent homes. Then the empty bathhouses will be remodeled into permanent housing.

By late evening the next day, the first bathhouse was up and operating and the first tents were set up. The very first load of residents arrived, and the cook tent had a buffet already set up for dinner.

Within this first load were Jacques, Pierre, Michel, and their families. Tagging along for the ride was a traveling clown show composed of Matt Ramon, George Rooney, and Brad

Kitt, who kept the bus entertained with their antics during the six-hour trip.

Dan, a hard-working, northern Indiana boy with the honest mentality typical of the mid-west, stood next to Stone. Both were feeling good about themselves after spending the last six months designing and perfecting the first bathhouse. Now the acid test was about to begin with an onslaught of Haitians who had been trapped in a bouncing bus for six hours with a group of professional clowns who kept sides splitting with laughter using jokes to tricks.

3...2...1, "And this is David Fallon coming to you live from sunny California while 3200 miles away in Ft. Liberte' Haiti the first bus load of new owners will be disembarking in just a few moments as we watch them take their first steps on the land they will call home for now on.

"The plan is to help them build a farm and manufacturing community that will offer them a home, food, education, clothing, and medical all for a cost equivalent of harvesting just 9 Tomatoes a Day. This is a dream come true for many of the people working on and for this project. The moment of truth has arrived, the hard work begins."

George Rooney jumped to the ground and began walking up to Stone to find out what they could do to help. Stone asked if they could go inside and help the people understand how to flush the toilets, afterward get everyone rounded up for dinner.

"George, George do you have your ear piece in? How was the trip George, this is David Fallon."

"Hi David, the trip was fine. We had lots of laughs. This was an excellent chance to get to know each other. I am excited about getting started in the morning. However, right now I have a little training to perform. Thanks for checking in."

With that George walked inside the bathhouse and started to make sure everyone knew that flushing was a courtesy; there were others that would follow and it is important to keep this area very clean for the health and safety of everyone. Washing hands must be done so germs are not spread to others.

Yes that is right, George as well as Matt and Kitt never gave a second thought to helping their new friends, learn to use modern conveniences. They had been to other parts of the world and seen the devastation that the lack of sanitation can do to an entire village. This had nothing to do with pride and image; it had everything to do with saving lives.

"Sunny called for the cameras to show the line of people but keep the light from the bathroom door to the right of the frame."

True to form, the clowns lined everyone up getting them prepared and informed how to use a toilet some have never seen. Matt stood outside with Jacques explaining what this new technology was about, and how it worked.

Kitt and George went inside to provide traffic control, and to reinforce Matt's potty training. Like caged monkeys, however, the clowns started to get bored and found a way to relieve that problem. Kitt pulled out some lighter fluid, poured it on George's backside, and set it on fire.

While Matt was still talking about how the toilet waste produced gas that was used for cooking, George came running out of the bathhouse screaming with his butt on fire. Matt's audience went quiet, their eyes and mouths wide open.

"George, are you ok? What is happening over there? Sunny, Stone are you there? This is David can anyone hear me? George seems to be on fire. What is happening?

While Rooney rolled on the ground, putting his fire out, Matt turned around and looked for Stone. Stone grabbed Dan by the arm and began leading him to the cook tent.

"David, this is Stone; it seems the boys just found a new way to relieve tension, while also calling attention to themselves. Boy those guys really know how to introduce a new technology to the world."

"From our position here Stone, things seemed to be going very wrong for a few seconds."

"David it will be interesting to see how their humor mixes with the deep rooted superstitions of these people. But this too shall pass, I am going to eat David, it has been a long day."

Everyone standing in line who had witnessed the clown running with his butt on fire started to head for the bushes instead. Kitt was on the porch holding his sides; red in the face from laughing. Matt, fearing for the success of the bathhouses, was trying to figure out how he should react. Seeing Stone slowly shaking his head as he walked away, Matt decided to match Kitt. In the light of day, perceptions will change.

Sunny was happy for the action. He caught it all on tape. It aired live to millions of viewers. "That's a wrap, let's call it a night. Susan, get that footage on YouTube tonight; it will be viral by morning. Our viewers will double." Sonny called to his staff to get some food then sleep. It will be an early morning. With that bit of fun concluded, everyone got fed and learned where their tent assignments were. They were all tired and needed sleep. In the morning, the work would begin. The clowns, Stone, Dan, Sunny, and Jacques, were sitting at the table having a drink and a cigar when Kitt started laughing again,

"Man, I am sorry, but I just couldn't help myself. I hope I didn't scare everyone so bad they will never use the toilets again." The laughter got infectious.

Stone smiled, "These people have been using holes in the ground and walking in mud mixed with crap for years. They have never had a bathhouse before. Now that they do, they will use them. Mothers care for their children's health that is all we can count on."

Everyone at the table got down to planning tomorrow's business. They agreed to split the people into three groups; each clown got his group and mission. Tomorrow, there would be more bathhouse construction and setting up of more tents so that all the families could get here as soon as possible. Over the next week, the other coaches would be arriving with their families.

Soon the planting would have to begin.

19

Field Planting – The Network Channel

The best inspiration offered to others comes from a place buried deep in your soul that sees light only in great times of need.

The farm tractors arrived and pointed to the area where they would begin plowing the fields. They would have to start soon. The crops must be harvested before the hurricane season begins or they would be lost to the heavy rains.

The rest of the bathhouses were built and the remaining tents were erected. The people had a dry place to sleep, sanitation, and a central cookhouse plus a medical facility. A tent served as the children's schoolhouse. Everyday the dream got closer to reality. Now the fields needed preparation and planting.

"Hey, hey, hey--HEY!" Tom Banks could be heard yelling towards the operator of a tractor, over the noise of the diesel motor, "No one is planning on planting crops in the road. Get back behind the grid! Behind the grid!" He commanded. "Stay within the lines!" he yelled once again. Tom turned away and started to mumble to himself, or at least he thought he was alone,

"Coloring books, lots of damn coloring books, and colored pencils also--Lots of them! It is not going to help that yahoo, but it will sure as hell teach the new kids to--STAY IN THE DAMN LINES! Listen to me, I'm talking to myself."

Sunny then called for the balloon Sky-cam 4 to pull back from Banks and ready to switch to Remy for a close up, "On my mark...1...2," As the camera lenses began to pull back, Banks turned and looked up spiking the camera located in the sky, the last words heard from Banks before Sunny cut to Remy was,

"Oh shit! You weren't recording that were you? You'd tell me when you were taping wouldn't you?"

...3 switch.

Remy Moore had her crew of one thousand planting coffee trees, coconut palms, and cocoa; all these trees plus plantain trees and mango trees were placed along the road-ways and in between the fields that would contain the crops.

David called over Remy's earpiece, as sky-cam 3 zoomed down filling the frame with her dirt and sweat covered outfit and floppy hat, "Remy, can you hear me?"

"Yes, I can David, what's up?"

"Just checking in to see how things are going over there?"

"David, everything is moving forward quickly. One thing I can say for sure, this will be the tastiest road ever built. I can see myself back here in the next few years picking and eating the fruits, regaining all the weight I am burning off this after-noon."

David laughed. "Alright Remy, stay safe and hydrated, from sky-cam 3 everything looks great." Before the shot was over Remy also spiked the camera smiling and held up a bot-tle of Fiji water, using it to wave hello, and goodbye.

In the past, product placements would help offset the production costs of filming. For the advertisers, the placements were subliminal suggestions to the viewers asking them to use the product as the actors did. They were a cheap advertising tool that lasted for generations. Product placements were different in this reality show. Whether the product was good for your health, bad for your health, or made your daily choirs easier, the advertisers were sending out another message; we cannot exist without each other, business is about more than profit, business is about survival. To survive a business must be part of humanities fabric. Helping to promote the reality show helps to promote the product, but it was as important to the company's Board of Directors, the management, and the employees that the more important message was loud and clear—our company cares!

Sean Glenn detractors criticized him for smoking Lucky Strikes during the taping of the show, giving them placement. Sean's reply was pure Sean, "I am an American, and we promote freedom of choice. I choose to put in my body what I want. Our government has made us fully aware of the dangers of smoking and if you noticed, I did not mince my words that cigarettes can kill you. As far as the morality of smoking my Strikes on this show, talk with the producers. As far as product placements go, I would shake hands with a Republican if it helps us meet the goal of building this farm."

A central bio-digester had to be constructed, which would begin converting animal and plant wastes into methane gas. Pre-digesters already existed near the bathhouses, and those were supplying gas to the cook tents and generators.

Normally, these waste streams would release into the environment tons of methane gas, which is a significant contributor to global warming, sometimes 10 to 20 times more harmful than carbon dioxide. Bio-digesters capture methane and other by-products normally thrown away and put them to good use.

Bio-solids high in nitrogen and phosphates are another by-product of the bio-digesters. The bio-solids are collected and spread over the fields in place of fertilizers. However, unlike the solids from typical city sewer plants, bio-solids from farm bio-digesters do not contain chemicals, pharmaceuticals, steroids, and other unhealthy contaminants.

By now, all ten teams had their groups organized. The team leaders had taken over the day-to-day operations. Getting the crops growing was priority number one. With crops coming in, the cooperative would become more independent each day.

Sean Donnelly was easy to locate. Each morning and every afternoon he would play the bagpipes, leading his troops to battle and then bringing them back home to celebrate the day's successes.

Sunny adored Donnelly's drama and used much of the footage to open and close that days programming.

Sean Glenn had no card tricks; that was not his style. He had lived in the tent cities with the victims of the earthquake and felt their pain. He knew the urgency they felt for getting their lives back on track. Any time Glenn emerged on camera, he was in a serious discussion with a crewmember, on the phone ordering supplies, raising money, or showing the workers he was not too good to get down in the dirt with them and plant when needed.

One hot afternoon, Forrest Whittier was having a small rebellion in his field of responsibility. His skills as a leader were to be tested. He had thirty disgruntled young males walking off the job site. Apparently, they had lost their focus and their vision. They were leaving the work for others to finish. Forrest drove up to them in his golf-cart and asked, "What's going on? We have crops to plant."

"We aren't your slaves!" yelled one of the angrier workers, "And we're tired of working for free! Nou se gade kochon mouted (We're fed up)!"

"Sunny screamed to his crew, "Zoom sky-cam 5 onto Forrest now! Turn the microphones on and shut-up…go!"

"Ho, Ho, Hold on there. Hold on right there, my friends! What did you call me? Did you tell me to put something up somewhere?" Forrest got out of the golf-cart, ambled over, and presented his towering frame to the group of young men.

"First, you aren't working for anyone but yourselves and your families. Second, you aren't getting paid because sweat is all you have to pay for your ownership in a piece of this business, and a place to live in; but hey, if you have the cash on hand, then by all means go buy something equivalent to this, and make room for someone who actually needs this opportunity."

"You ain't got it man." Complained another, "Travay se tout sa nou fe' isit la (work is all we do here)."

"Everyone has to work hard in the beginning no matter what they are doing. Even an airplane has to work hard before it defeats gravity," Forrest explained. "No matter what, you have to work hard on anything before it starts to become a little easier. Farming is no different. Food doesn't just jump out of the ground and into your bowl."

Forrest knelt down while picking up a handful of dirt. "Everything exists within a cycle, and we are right here in the middle living it. We are not nomads foraging on anything that happens to come our way. We are farmers; we work the land to survive and to gain more control of our futures.

"The Earth gives us soil full of the stuff that's needed to give life. We till it, plant it, water it, and protect it. Then with luck and prayer, it yields a bounty. Here, on this farm, you eat the harvest and then process your waste back into Earth's soil and once again, the cycle begins when you plant your next meal.

"Yes, its work, and no, you do not get paid until your work yields its fruit. That is the price of freedom. That is the price of ownership. Work is what we have to do to stay alive; playing, art, singing, dancing, and girls is what we do to *be* alive. If you do not want to be someone's slave, then get your butts back to work. If you do not, you will forever be dependent on crumbs falling off someone else's table."

Forrest stood up and began to walk back to the golf-cart. "There are no chains here or straw-bosses. Each of you is your own boss. If you want to quit, then go sign out and leave the cooperative. If you want to stay, then get back to your jobs."

The young men looked at each other, shrugged, and then slowly walked back to begin planting once more, but this time with the beginnings of a different outlook. Each person was still adjusting to the concept that a Haitian could be his own boss. This was too good to be true. In the past, there had been so many unfulfilled promises: too many lies.

For the moment, the happiness quota had risen a little higher for everyone. Forrest had done more good with his two-minute pep talk than all the prior lectures.

The same Turks that were ready to walk off the job began to repeat Forrest's words to the others: work was viewed, once again, with purpose and hope; the feeling of being back in control of one's future invigorated the farmers. Because of the visible progress, infectious enthusiasm spread between the film crews, the celebrities, and the volunteers.

Sunny sent interviewers with cameras to talk with the young people to learn more about them, and how they were feeling after Forrest's speech.

To be sure, feeding ten thousand families every morning, afternoon and evening is a monumental task for anyone. Worrying that someone might go to bed at night hungry can take its toll on the strongest of leaders, but sharing the responsibility among ten thousand owner/workers would reduce each person's burden by ten thousand fold.

Still it took strong leadership to stay the course. Timetables were critical. For instance, it would be important not to slaughter the animals too early. Some were needed for breeding, and others needed nourishing to yield the greatest amount of protein.

Try telling that, however, to children who are crying because their extended bellies are empty and they are sick from eating the only things they have in front of them, dirt and grass. The rice and beans provided by US Aid and other groups could go only so far. They became a commodity more valuable than gold; they were, in fact, life itself. Fully aware of this, armed gangs soon popped up to make a living stealing food from orphanages and warehouses. Eventually, the repackaged goods ended up back in the street markets.

Protecting the supplies had become as big a priority as planting the fields. The site plan considered security, but the backhoes had to get there first before the multi-purpose rim ditches could provide the critical barriers to entry.

Pierre had formed a small group of volunteers that patrolled the ten pods where the food is stored. Each person had a radio; each was able to help the other within minutes of a call to action. There had been attempts to steal the food, but all from gangs housed outside the cooperative. All the attempts quickly failed when the massive presence of Pierre emerged from the darkness. Sometimes all it took was the knowledge that he was just minutes away.

The planting was taking shape. Over 4000 acres of land had been plowed. A sea of bodies was in the field planting. Wherever possible, much of the work was done with farm equipment donated by American corporations. This left many people searching for more work. It was time to start building homes.

20

Building homes – The Network Channel

Giving an artist an opportunity means giving him paint, brushes, and a canvas. Creating the image only makes him a beggar.

For two weeks, thousands of shipping containers filled with building materials, had been rolling in. These materials would supply the mega-effort needed to house 50,000 people in 2500 quads. The first challenge of getting the fields prepared and the crops growing was well underway. People now needed to build the homes. The skilled labor identified from the entry applications was culled from the farm labor. Unskilled labor had to remain in the field for maintenance operations.

Perhaps there is a very subtle but important point, to be discussed here, concerning skilled and unskilled labor. On the farm, everything and everyone had a purpose. So as each person learned the importance of their job and learned to do it well, they became more valuable to the expansion of the farm cooperative concept and network. When these workers are trained fully, they could relocate to other farms that are just getting started and take on a more responsible supervisory job. With this in mind, the most ambitious of the group began to learn as many of the job disciplines as they could. Unskilled labor quickly turned into skilled and soon elevated to expert. This created teaching opportunities that created even more after hour jobs. Instead of sitting at home at night, workers went to school to learn.

The primary point being you could be a highly skilled carpenter one day, the next you could have a potato rake in your hands clearing weeds. The Haitians say, "Ou pa gen pi enpo'tan Le' sa a, travay la kit a dwe fini (You are no more important than the job that must be done).

Foundations were being dug and were ready to be poured. Everyone pitched in. A small concrete plant had been built, and there was a steady supply of concrete trucks. The crews could not get too far ahead in case the rains started, but the foundations were falling into place quickly.

Rubble from Port-au-Prince had been put through a giant grinder that created the aggregate for the concrete. The concrete foundations were poured and allowed to cure for 5 days.

Next, foam blocks were laid up so that concrete could fill them in the coming days. It takes less than a day for a crew of eight to install these. The foam blocks yield multiple benefits: they have a high insulation rating, they act as forms for concrete, they are inexpensive, and they have a high sound deadening effect.

The plumbing and wiring were installed, as the blocks were laid up. With everything in place, the concrete trucks would return to begin pouring the walls. Rebar was used to tie together the foundations, the walls, and the roof trusses.

Each house is designed to withstand winds of at least 200 miles an hour. The foundations are raised to avoid flooding. The concrete and roofing materials were selected to resist the termites and mold that are such fundamental inconveniences in the tropics. Earthquakes cannot bring these flexible structures down. There would be no more nightmares.

The roofs are metal with thin-film solar panels pre-installed. The roofing segments snap together quickly, becoming wind and water-resistant. An exhaust fan draws cool air, in from the porch, and blows hot air, out the attic.

When the house is plumbed, and is dried-in with doors and windows, the crews connect the homes to the remote monitoring system that regulates gas, electric, and water; plus displays on a screen, the work assignments for the next two weeks: The same system IBM will tie into with their farm wide scheduling and economics software.

TJ had his crew working hard laying out the irrigation on the putting greens. Remy was installing trees along the fairways, as fast as the fairways were constructed and the trees could be delivered.

Sunny zoomed sky-cam 5 down towards TJ. David Fallon wanted to check in with TJ; more so, because David wanted a scoop that would get all the news agencies talking.

"TJ can you hear me, this is David Fallon speaking."

"I hear you fine David, what's going on?"

"Just checking in TJ, to see how long you think it will take before I can play a round of golf with you there in Haiti."

"Grass grows quickly here. There is great soil and lots of water so I estimate about six weeks from now you can have a go at me."

"How many points will you spot me?"

"David, if I keep playing the way I have over the last few weeks, you may have to spot me some points."

"So TJ, I have not had a chance to interview you to ask why you decided to help build this course in Haiti: can you take the time to discuss those reasons with us now?"

"This is difficult to talk about, but it is a lesson that sooner or later I wanted to share, so now is as good as any other.

"A few years ago I was at the top of my game. I simply could do no wrong. But I wanted to do better. I wanted to be the best there ever was: so, I hired a swing coach. After watching me for a few tournaments, he took me to dinner and told me if I wanted to be great, I had to change my swing. Other than that advice, he told me there was little more he could offer.

"I took his advice to mean that I should literally change my swing. Therefore, I began to practice using a new swing style. Night and day, I practiced a new swing. Just as I was beginning to perfect that swing, the car crash happened and the newspapers pretty much told you the rest.

"During my divorce, I had a lot of personal time to reflect. I was embarrassed. I let my wife and, worse yet, my children down. I let my success and financial rewards get the best of me. I was raised differently than the way I was living. I lost my center. Just because I could do something, right or wrong, I did it. I did these things without thinking about the people who raised me, the people who depended on me, or those who looked to me as an example. I was selfish.

"My game suffered because I was suffering a loss of identity. I was no longer on the fairways playing with a million fans, I was there suffering through a game on my own. I had not only lost my standing in the sport, I had lost my self-respect.

"When a friend told me about this opportunity I did not even hesitate. I knew this was an opportunity to help others, and whether or not I got my game back, I was not going to let my skills go to waste. I jumped on this job and have not looked back since.

"So now when I look back at what my coach said, I understand why he left and could not offer more help. If I wanted to be the best, I had to change my swing; in other words, I had to change my choices and my lifestyle. I was already the number one golfer: I simply had to choose to be a better person: to be the best the world has ever known.

"What I went through, any addict would understand. Everyday, I have to wake up and remind myself this is a new day and I have to start all over again. I check my ego and then go to work.

"I will always love golf and I am not going anywhere. But I am going to be a winner one way or the other; either on the golf course; or, here building golf courses on these eco-farms. I got my mojo back and I will continue to work on my swing."

"Wow TJ, I don't know what anyone else is thinking, but I can only say I am proud to know you. I know if you could change the past, you would; but it takes a bigger man to accept the past while building a better future. Good luck and thank you for the help, I look forward to competing against you."

"Helicopter-cam, are you in position?"

"Yes, Sunny we are."

"If you will, see if you can zoom away from TJ and put the entire golf course in your frame, now please."

What TJ and Sunny were about to show the world was remarkable.

ESPWA

(HOPE)

21

Product Development – The Design Channel

The problem with a throwaway society is that good ideas and profit margin are also tossed out.

The management team and product development experts collected around the conference table to discuss future efforts and products. The primary agenda items involved what commodities will immediately feed the people, and at the same time create value added opportunities that would generate farm profits. "Meals Ready to Eat (MRE)" was at the top of the agenda, first because of their demand, but mostly because a portion of the production could be set aside for emergencies that would threaten the survival of the ownership. Next consideration was given to soymilks, dairy products, oats, rice, and cereals that could be produced and stored without the use of refrigeration. Finally the discussions shifted to how canning lines could be financed that would preserve and add value to seasonal vegetables and fruits.

The camera lights were on but David did not want to break the flow of the engineer's discussions: so he and the audience just listened.

Buildings were planned that would act as farmers markets and/or processing plants where value would be added to the harvested commodities. Manufacturers had already called to inquire about private labeling if quality control and shipping guarantees were assured.

Tabasco peppers would be easy to grow and would not take up a lot of land. Bottlers were happy to hand over their labels, packaging, and recipes in return for a larger profit margin, increased production, and organic labeling.

Rabbits are a fast-growing source of protein and have many uses. The meat is sold fresh, or frozen in biodegradable packaging. The furs could go to a tannery and then to a sewing shop where designers could create patterns for winter wear to be sold in Europe, Asia, and the USA. The by-products fed the pigs. The urine and pellets from the rabbits charge the bio-digester.

Pork yields meat, sausage links and patties, and ground meat. Pig waste would be the principal generator of methane fuels in the bio-digester.

Chickens would yield eggs and meat. Feathers fill pillows and adorn craft projects. The processing byproducts feed the pigs. Their body wastes enter the bio-digesters.

Dairy Cows and goats yield dairy products such as milk, butter, cream, yogurt, sour cream, ice cream, cheese, meat, and leather goods.

All the bio-solids from the bio-digesters are tilled into the soils, eliminating the need for expensive fertilizers. The liquid fertilizers are mixed with gray water, and the used for irrigation in green houses and on the crops.

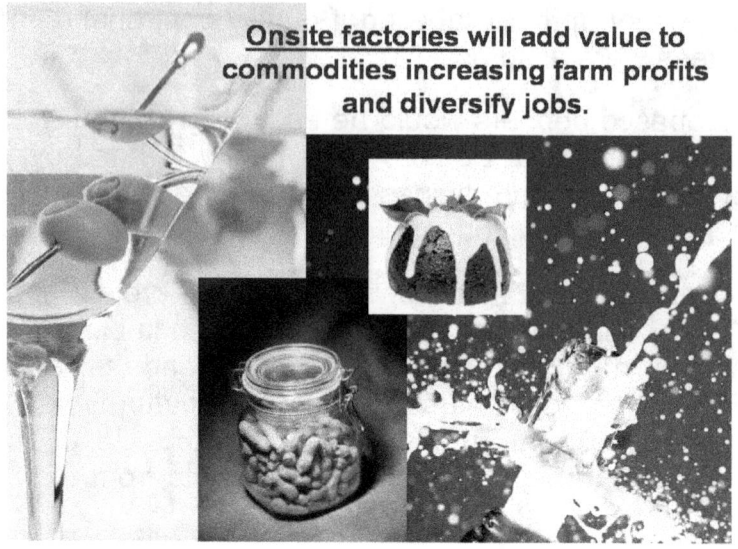

Onsite factories will add value to commodities increasing farm profits and diversify jobs.

Some governments had already given the food processing plant, purchase orders to manufacture meals ready to eat (MRE rations) for disaster and war torn areas. This justified the purchase of the ovens and vacuum sealing machines required for the process. At this point, the engineers and management felt that, should nature or man rain down a disaster, they could quickly recover without outside help.

Coffee unique to the Ft. Liberte' Mountain areas would be harvested, packaged, and branded.

Cocoa would be collected, processed, and branded into a healthy organic dark chocolate for worldwide distribution. The blending of vanilla beans, natural sea salts, and cane sugar all grown on the farm could yield a new globally competitive product line.

Tomatoes would be grown organically and allowed to ripen on the vine. This allows all the natural sugars to develop, a process that does not happen in the tomatoes for which consumers now pay $4 USD a pound in American markets.

Kenaf grows wildly in the overflow discharge of the farm waters. The kenaf plants polish the water, removing all nitrogen, phosphates, and silt before it finally enters the pristine waters of Liberte' Bay. The leaves feed livestock. The stalks are shredded and made into rope, high-grade stationery, and durable textiles.

Fields of Sugarcane and Kenaf served as the first line of defense for good water quality. The cane supplied raw materials for sugars, syrups, and rums. The stalks ground-up created bagasse used as filler for livestock feed, or bedding for chickens. Afterwards, the waste filled bio-digesters to create more methane.

Jacques learned how to sell supply contracts to major grocers, and to find designers wanting their visions for leather and fur turned into commercial products. His years on the street made him a very affable salesperson capable of interpreting changes in voice tone during phone conversations. This allowed him to know when he was losing a prospect's interest; he learned to adapt his pitch quickly. Pre-sales and supply contracts were mounting quickly under his efforts.

Trade barriers set up by the northern states like America, England, and other European Countries began to breakdown. The vision of a collection of farm cooperatives began to take hold and their power began to be felt. If the northern states wanted to sell their products to these new consumers in the cooperative, they had to open their doors to the products that would come out of them. The American consumer benefited from the increased competition, seeing significantly lower food costs at the market. The larger corporate owned farms started sending lobbyists to Washington to pressure Congress for stricter trade barriers. Consumer advocates lobbied to reduce barriers because of the obvious lower costs at the retail level. One Congressman stated on a morning show that the future for big corporate owned farms looked bleak. With lower costs came less profits and that is all the corporations were concerned about. Therefore, it was likely they would be getting out of the farm business eventually. Asked if that was a bad thing the Congressman replied, "Absolutely not. That loss would usher back in the small farmers, which have always been the backbone of American agriculture. More so, it would open-up a niche for the Haitian model for farm cooperatives here in America, helping to put people back in homes and back to work. How can that be a bad thing? When the cost burden of education, medical, and housing is taken off the shoulders of the government and but on the shoulders of owners of the cooperative that is sound capitalistic economics."

Streets were landscaped with coffee, mango, and banana, plus citrus, and cocoa: all trees that sequester carbon and generate a cash crop. Flowering plants create beautiful landscapes; but they also have other purposes. Flowers support a thriving bee population that would help pollinate the crops while producing a viable honey yield as another important product.

The rim ditches and ponds were filled with fish that were caught by the farmers and eaten for dinner, or ground up by the farm and used to supplement livestock feed.

The organic wastes from all the homes were collected in separate trashcans and used to supplement livestock feed. Cans, paper, bottles, and plastics went to the recycling and processing plant, where the methane fuels helped turn them back into packaging for value-added products.

Nutrient rich bio-solids from the digesters were stored in piles and mixed with other biodegradable products such as paper or cardboard: there was no need for landfills everything was used.

Above this pile of compost were large birdhouses. On the top were "bird condos" occupied by at least three native species. Below the condos was habit for bats, thousands upon thousands of them. During the night, they would leave to eat the flying insects that would otherwise lay eggs on the crops. If the insect eggs hatched, the application of pesticides was required to kill the insect larva. Bats greatly reduced the need for pesticides. Bats were natural pest control. In addition, during the day their guano mixed with the compost pile significantly increasing the amount of nutrients it contained. The higher nutrient content allowed the compost to be spread further across the crops. Worms in the compost pile helped to expedite the breakdown of paper products. The worms also left castings that would turn sandy nutrient poor soils into a rich resource for growing crops. When there were too many worms, the excess went to the chickens.

During the day, the chickens roamed in the fields finding insects to eat. At dusk, they would return to the safety of the pens, where food and water was also plentiful.

At dusk, the bats would blacken the sky like a swarm of locus. Eventually this would become a tourist attraction: A gathering place where the locals could make additional money by selling rum drinks and handcrafted merchandise to eco-tourists that came to admire nature working for the benefit of itself, and for humanity.

The entire farm process ended with a clean discharge into the bays that yielded fresh, unpolluted seafood. Wherever water stopped, or was pumped from the ground, it was used multiple times and each use created value by growing a plant, supporting a human being or farm animal, or helped to create fuels that would power the farm and industry. The entire production cycle was a nearly closed sustainable loop that generated profit.

"Jean-Baptist this is David, we have been watching in amazement all the things the farm is doing. I cringe at the waste we produce here in America and how little care there is about the billions of dollars of potential revenues we simply let rot-away. Is there a way we can turn things around in this country?"

"David everything can be turned around, all it takes is will power and the desire of someone to do it. The difference between our two countries is that here in Haiti we have no choice. We have no lands we can waste for landfills. Moreover, we have very little in the way of raw materials, so it is important for us to use everything we can, as many times as we can. Have no worries David, America will catch up with Haiti one day soon. Then you too will not have a choice.

"And David, we have not discussed the multiple benefits of building farm cooperatives other than lifting people out of poverty: take a look at this slide before we sign off and just consider how these farms could change our current political landscape. The only groups that will not support this program are those that build machines of war."

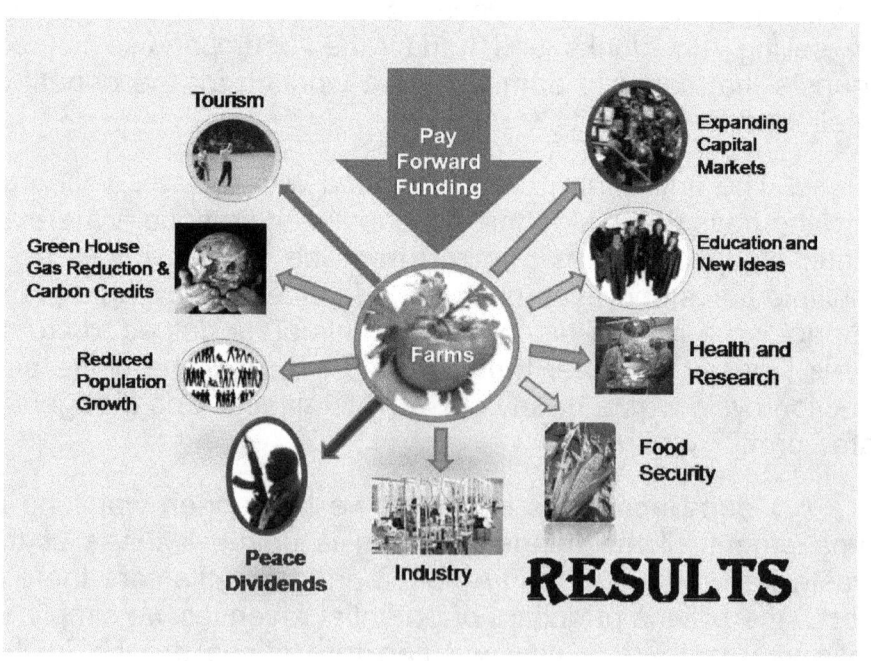

22

Building Factories and Commercial Space

The equation does not require rocket science; factories go where they can get the most help for the best cost and find the cheapest resources to build products that consumers want.

As the farms progressed and excitement grew, more manufacturers, clothing designers and food processors all wanted to get in on the ground floor of Haiti's new growth. The game show demonstrated to them how stable the country had become and how powerful the forces were that stood behind the redevelopment efforts.

History, however, still got in the way of Haiti's future. In the past foreigners, but more specifically white men, could not own land in Haiti. This law's origins were rooted in the curse of slavery and the hard won battles fought for freedom. It was now time, as the world realized, to put history aside, and start finding how we can grow together. The fear that whites would purchase all the choice lands and own the best factories would have to be framed in national policies that would develop in the years to come. At this moment, the priority was the farms, food, housing, and the factory jobs that would begin to build up around the farming cooperatives.

Bellevue had called an emergency meeting. He proposed irrevocable changes to the constitution and government policies that would protect landownership for outside investors. One stipulation was that the sale of land to outsiders had to be approved by the government and that approval or denial would be completed within 60 days from the day a complete application was made.

Even without the new laws, risk tolerant entrepreneurs built new factories outside the farm property. They would take advantage of the new commodities and would add value to them as they ripened; something that had not been allowed to happen for over 240 years.

Additionally, free trade zones circumvented those government officials that would disguise their corruption as taxes and tariffs

Besides the hectic work Tom Banks was doing with the farmers, he spent a lot of his free time on the phone multi-tasking with the CEOs of companies in which he was an investor. He had convinced them of the opportunities that now exist in Haiti and had persuaded them to reallocate some of their production from China to Haiti. They were taking advantage of the diversity of crops that would result in new food and clothing product lines and of the cheaper shipping costs to American markets. Chinese manufacturers were also beginning to look at factories in Haiti for the same reason.

One factory was being set up to assemble solar panels in the hope that they could capture a major portion of the new Haitian markets and the other Caribbean markets as well. Middle Eastern oil producers anticipated the future and began to invest in factories that would refine vegetable oils into bio-fuels.

Remy Moore was also multi-tasking. She had convinced her partners that a Hard Rock Café would do well next to the new resort hotel built on the beachfront to house the celebrities and film crews.

Others had convinced a large luxury boat builder that relocating to Liberte' Bay was in its best interest.

US AID in partnership with the World Bank had fronted a loan to build a new port that could accommodate cruise lines stopping over. Additionally, improvements to the Cape Haitian International Airport and the connector roads to the new cooperative were funded.

Haitian innovators had found new production methods that would make it possible to use Kenaf and other hemp plant species as a replacement for oil based fiberglass and resins.

Like a field of sunflowers, the farm in Liberte' Bay was beginning to bloom and the flowers were making decisions that followed the sun's brightness, instead of the pasts darkness.

23

Harvest – The Network Channel

Playful competition yields great art.

The darkness of night started to give way to the sun rising over the mountains to the east. There was excitement in the air. The fields were ripe and ready to yield their fruits, and the animals were content and fat.

Sean Donnelly awoke with an air of victory about him that only a highland Scot could understand. This morning he would make an impression. He dressed in his finest clan attire, picked up his bagpipes, and headed for his tea.

Everyone in the cantina eyed him with cautiousness, not quite knowing how to react to his dress. Putting his empty teacup down, he marched smartly to the staging area and began to play his pipes. The cameras were rolling, and the producers sat down in astonishment.

As the farmers began to gather, he turned and walked toward the field with the glow of the morning Sun turning him into a silhouette against the high vegetation. The farmers in tow had their baskets, and it was time to gather their victory.

Sunny let out a sigh saying, "and God said let there be goose bumps."

Jimmy Muffet was sitting in a golf cart watching all this drama and he simply said, "Show off," under his breath. Muffet didn't fancy being a part of Donelly's backdrop.

In retaliation, at noon, Muffet had the Coral Briefers set up on a flatbed truck. Jimmy drove it out into the field and handed out sandwiches and water to his crew. Then the entire band jumped on their instruments and started playing a concert that lasted an hour and a half. Five hundred people were dancing, laughing, and smiling. The harvesting teams in the far distance were distracted.

Even though there remained a language barrier for most, notes and rhythm bridged them all. By the end of the show, the farmers were fired up and ready to start loading up their harvest. The Margarita Dozer had done his job. The Workers had become oblivious to the hot Sun and the fact that their muscles ached to the bone.

Before leaving the microphone, Jimmy yelled towards Donnelly's team "Take that, you moss-munching, skirt-wearing highlander!" Jimmy never took to the idea of obtaining a knighthood anyway; he had no fear of a Scottish reprisal. Besides, he just could not understand the concept of a man wearing a dress in public giving a bag of pipes a blowjob. But then again, what did he know anyway.

One could imagine Sean taking umbrage about the skirt comment and mumble under his breath, "The damn manatee banger." Nothing was in anger, in the end the revelries were all in good fun.

The others did not partake in the drama. They simply put on gloves and dug in with the rest of the farmers. Getting the harvest to market was their primary and only goal. The farmers took note of the celebrities' sweat and determination. From the start, the farmers had no idea who these great American movie stars were; for now they only know them for the leaders they had become in their own world.

The children of the celebrities and even some of the spouses showed up to help. It was in stark contrast to Hollywood, and the kids would carry the experience with them into adulthood.

Others from around the Haitian nation started to show up to learn about this new farming program. It had become a backdrop for would be parliamentary leaders and perhaps presidents. One such person was the entertainer Mickey. He had been working with Sean Glenn trying to get a better handle on the complexities of the farm, to learn how the efforts here could spread to other regions. He was a fine listener.

24

The Winner – The Network Channel

Everyone wins when no one loses... That should be a song.

An amazing thing happened even with a million dollar prize on the line. Rooney's team had its trucks loaded; they needed only to drive to the market for their prize. They were first in line, with eight other teams in close pursuit, but ahead of them, they saw what could be a real disaster. Kitt's trucks had somehow turned over, and all their harvest was scattered. Instead of blowing by, something out of the ordinary began to take place: first, they stopped.

Sunny called for sky-cam 4 to turn and zoom in on the disaster and then to listen in.

Rooney got out of his truck and leaned against it. He looked at Kitt and smiled. Then he called for his team to jump out and help. They took out ropes to right their competitor's trucks and pull them out of the mud. After accomplishing that, they began to help them reload.

Kitt had always been two steps ahead of Rooney, and he never missed a chance to let him know it. This time, Kitt looked at Rooney and nodded with a smile. He was bested and worse yet by a gentleman. Sometimes you can set some-one's butt on fire, and it does not even take a match.

Two other groups also stopped and helped. Everybody got out of the trucks to help reload Kitt's overturned trucks. Other workers ran over to help. Before everyone knew it, the teams had the trucks reloaded and they were waiting for each other to restart the race.

"Kitt this is David, are you ok?"

"Awe we're just fine thanks. The tires slide on the mud and rolled the trucks into the ditch. Some of the other guys stopped to help right the trucks and to help us reload."

"Kitt that is pretty nice of them, but what about the con-test? Are they giving up a chance of beating you?"

"You best talk to George about that."

"David, this is George, you thinking that if I don't get there first I will be a loser? You calling us losers Dave?"

The last big surprise of this entire grueling game had nothing to do with money or winning; it was all about helping each other push forward--many tribes of many colors learning that self-interest can be enhanced by cooperation.

All the trucks entered the market at the same time. The music started to blare, and cameras began to flash. All were winners, including strangers from the other side of the world, because a business model had been proven. Now it only had to mature and spread.

And so was born a new way of conducting global busi-ness that would pull hundreds of millions if not billions of peo-ple out of poverty. Multinational corporations had learned how to achieve their marketing goals while also achieving a mean-ingful and lasting purpose with their advertising dollars. Corpo-rations that did not adopt this new advertising goal would be left in the lurch.

The new standard for a successful reality show became one that resulted in purpose shrouded by entertainment, not mindless dribble.

"This is David Fallon and the hosts of 9 Tomatoes a Day thanking you for helping to build homes and a farm for 10,000 families, 50,000 people, who were once living in the squalor of a tent city. Be sure to make plans to go visit the 'New Hope,' you helped to build. God bless you and until our next big adventure together, good night."

25

Gravy

Every heart contains a poet.

The three young Haitian friends ran to their favorite pond and sat on the benches to begin what had become a nightly ritual. They had come a long way, given that they had almost lost their lives. In their own right, each had become men to admire.

Now the cameras and crews were gone, the sky started to signal the beginning of their favorite time of the day, a time when the tropical air gets cooler, the world begins to change colors, and the stars seemingly pop out of nowhere to witness them talking about their hopes and dreams.

Jacques stood up, spreading his arms like wings, turning in circles, and he said, "I want a huge jet plane so I can fly to any place in the world where I want to go, with gold and diamonds to make me shine for the ladies." Jacques had excelled in learning the produce trade and the secrets of becoming a successful sales person. He had also learned how to negotiate and became one of the most effective buying agents. He was still learning how to tone down his measure of success.

Pierre had worked hard in the fields and took training classes at night to learn law enforcement. At night instead of sleeping, he would go on patrols and help protect the farm from outside influences, which had been many. Over the year, Pierre had been shot twice and both times his massive size proved more durable than a simple lead bullet. Pierre leaned back, looking up to the sky," I want a big house with a limousine to take me and my beautiful wife and children anywhere we desire. And you, Michel, what do you want?"

Michel, who took to farming like a fish to water, looked towards the ground with a slight smile and bent down; scooping up earth with his hands. He rolled his thumbs in it. He felt a different type of energy surge through him rising from the dirt and followed by a glow that only a lover can provide. Dirt had always been his nemesis before; now it had become a part of him, just like an arm or leg. "Gravy, I only need gravy: If I do not get it that is ok, too."

Jacques screamed out, "Are you mad, Michel? We're dreaming here; you can have anything in the world you want, and you ask for gravy?"

Unknown to anyone especially Michel his hardened heart had softened in this world of toil and safety. He was able to breathe again and he began to realize the better natures of the people he now lived with. His poet had begun to awaken. Michel turned to look over the crops springing from the ground he had helped to plant, and more crops that he would soon harvest. The sunset colored the sky in a palette of swirling reds, blues, greens, and yellows, and a misty fog started to roll down the mountains. "I have lived in the streets, in plastic bags. I have awakened rolling in mud soaked in the urine and feces of ten thousand people. I have dug into trashcans to help find food for my family. I have watched a thousand dead people rot in the cracks of the Earth. I have choked on the stench of diesel fumes mixed with human flesh. I have worked for lifetimes only to get pennies that only buy more hunger.

"But now, I have my meat and potatoes: a clean, dry home for my family, a soft bed to sleep in, food every day and night, clean dirt to walk in and fresh water to drink, and I have my nine tomatoes a day to pay for these things. I own a dream.

"I work for myself, and my work combined with others' brings me and my family safety and happiness. If I want more, I merely have to work more. Gravy, that is all anyone could expect beyond these gifts; just gravy. Every breath I take and every step I dance from now on is gravy.

"Don't you see? Complete strangers, connected to us only by air and history, reached out like brothers and sisters giving us, and a million others, a gift of opportunity. I do not want to waste the balance of my gifts on glitter, I want to pound my feet into this Earth and leave meaningful footprints for others to see and follow; and if just a little gravy falls from the sky as a result of my hard work, that is ok, too."

In the background the music started to get louder near the cook tents, the nightly celebration once again ignited with the tossing of a few heads and the bumping of hips in response to the notes that danced off the trees and the evening breeze. Community was once again coming alive. Smiles had replaced the harsh memories of the past.

The three friends took note of the building excitement and ran to the event that was unfolding, they jumped into the ocean of dancing bodies held together by unseen glue made of rhythm and hope; and just then, it felt like God too was smiling.

26

The President Speaks

If my life has been wasted Lord, then I ask selfishly again if I am worthy of your grace.

In the morning, a formal celebration began with a tribute to the past and present. Michelin Louise-Perrier was the honored speaker. In attendance were the Haitian President, his cabinet, ministers, and members of the Parliament. Representatives from Spain, England, France, and many African Countries were there to honor the Haitian achievements. The world was watching in amazement.

The morning Sun was bright, and the smells of the farm soothing, reminding everyone that life and hope are all around us when cultivated by planning and work.

Madame Louise-Perrier walked to the podium. Her regal nature and posture projected Haiti's pride and honor to the world. News cameras were turning and the spotlights aimed to reflect every moment. This was Haiti's second largest victory. This was the second war Haiti had won while fighting for freedom; the first was against slavery, this one was against poverty. The northerners who had been their taskmasters in both wars had become their liberators in these last moments.

"Haiti has walked a jagged path," she began. "It has tripped and fallen many times. It has stood up for freedom and thrown off the chains of slavery.

"But we cannot forget that where we are today is not without the evil rained upon us by some and the unselfish force of good that has been poured upon us by many. Because we are the first to benefit from a new program whose mission is to expand past our shores in support of others who need help, let me share with you a story of forgiveness and hope.

"John Newton was an English youth who defied law and order. He was a disobedient sailor who could make up words and thoughts so ugly he would make his captain and crewmates cringe. He deserted the Royal Navy and was later caught and traded to a slave ship. He himself became a slave in Sierra Leone until his father bailed him out. He was a vile youth, a poor excuse for a human being.

"One night at sea there was a severe storm; men were being washed overboard. During the height of the storm, Newton cried out, 'If this life will not do, then the Lord have mercy upon us'! As the storm subsided, he did not forget the words. He began to ask if he and the life he had led were worth God's mercy.

"In the following years, he became a captain of slave ships, but fate soon took him away from that awful trade.

"He began to mellow, and his heart began to fill with a compassion he had never known before. He studied theology and later wanted to be ordained but was refused because he was known to consort with Methodists.

"Then, on one inspired day in 1772, he wrote down words that rang out from a deep corner of his soul. *Amazing Grace how sweet the sound that saved a wretch like me...*

"A short time after, in 1791, the slaves of Haiti began their fight for freedom and obtained it soon after.

"Newton's life mission became to break down hardened hearts and heal broken ones. He became an abolitionist and teamed with William Wilberforce to pass the Slave Trade Act of 1807.

"Today marks another milestone for Haiti. It is a time when the world has stepped up to help in a meaningful way to build a program intended to lift anchor here and sail around the globe in search of people in need of opportunity and dignity, and to correct yesterday's wrongs. A program that builds a stronger tomorrow for everyone while mending yesterdays sadness: an accomplishment greater than landing on the moon, for here humanity has opened their hearts and minds to over come fear and prejudice that will one day help us reach the stars. Haiti has become Hope's proving ground that a common purpose and a common vision for tomorrow will unite us all.

"There is no longer a need to seek apologies or forgiveness for the past. We need only look into our mirrors, acknowledge our humanity and that we are capable of rising above our lower natures, and accept the Amazing Grace that God offers us all. It has been proven on this soil.

"It is time we all stop using misguided quotes from what should be holy books as a measuring stick as to who gets to be equal, and instead use the compassion and words of God located only in our hearts to make and enforce a higher law that benefits everyone; most of all the least among us."

With that, Louise-Perrier walked over and took the hand of Prime Minister Bellevue. They stood side by side, their free hands waving to the applauding crowd. These two titans were to face off in the forthcoming election, competing to become the next President of Haiti. Bellevue bent over to pull up a man with a big smile and a shinny hairless head so he too could bask in the glory of the moment. He was also a contender for the presidential office, but he was a long shot at best: it was once again Mickey, the entertainer.

No one cared who won the vote. They would be there for each other, no matter the outcome, to influence Haiti's future, just as they had done in their government's darkest hour. Cooperation was finally realized to be in everyone's self-interest. This day, American politics could learn from Haiti.

Next, Former American President Clinton took the stage. "Generations from now," he began, "when humanity has been driven into space ships set out to colonize new worlds in order to ensure the survival of our species, history will show that the unity of all nations, plus justice and compassion for the least among us started here, at a cost of just 9 Tomatoes a Day. It was here in Haiti that humanity was shown a demonstration of a common purpose and how to live together. God bless Haiti, God bless America, and God bless all of Humanity."

Donnelly, decked out once again in his grand clan attire, took the stage without saying a word and began playing Amazing Grace on his bagpipes. In the proudest Scottish tradition, he marched from one end of the stage to the other.

Jimmy Muffet began to back him up with the organ, then the trumpets, horns, and strings followed. Few did not appreciate the depth of the moment, and few were without cloudy eyes. Everyone felt the need to be touching another beside him or her. A chain of humanity, which might one day make the solitary hero obsolete, was being formed without inducement except for an inspiration felt only within the moment. Perhaps it was initiated by a lone match lit months ago; or perhaps through the meeting of many lives swimming in the confluence of streams all rushing towards a common resting place. Later, Donnelly declared that it was his grandest time in the sun.

The farm animals had been watered and fed, but the rest of the work would have to wait. This day was set aside for art and celebration.

That evening, Sean Glenn jumped into the cockpit of the *Spiritus* with Stone: Lighting up a cigar and taking a swig of Jim Beam, Sean looked over the moon lit, glimmering waters of Liberte' Bay. "Why did you do it, Stone?" he asked. "What caused you to get into this wild and crazy ride?"

Stone looked at Sean, "Why the hell did you do it: Especially you? You have everything you need. You don't need this misery in your life."

Sean took another swig of Jim Beam, "I needed this misery more than most. It is only by taking on another's misery that you can learn how little yours matters. I do have everything I want and need. So I wanted to use my skills helping others to learn how to provide for themselves."

Stone was gazing off into the horizon, "After my company tanked, and after waking up for 90 straight days in what seemed like a never ending episode of groundhog day, I asked God, 'What do you want me to do? What the hell, do you want me to do**?** I don't even believe in a god.**'**

But a god still replied, "What do *you* want to do?"

I said, "I want to make a difference."

God replied, "Ok, so *make* a difference."

Stone continued, "The Universe never gives you an answer; it only puts opportunities in front of you. Then it asks, 'What are you going to do with this?' It took me a while to understand, but it came to me when it was needed.

"Haiti has always been on my punch list of problems I wanted to help find answers for: Especially when I saw a news program showing Haitian children eating cookies made from dirt, olive oil, and lemon. I made some. Take it from me; do not try that at home.

"When the earthquake happened, I knew I could develop a plan for the relocation of those millions of people, but they needed more, they needed a package deal.

"I had my business in Port Canaveral, Florida and spent a lot of time at a restaurant called Rusty's. For a time during my company's downturn, drinking there felt like being on the stage during a scene from *The Iceman Cometh*. There, my friend Tom told me about the work he was doing in Haiti with US AID and what a mess it had become. I could not get the idea out of my head that this had become my purpose.

"I knew the Haitians needed a complete package that would lead them out of yesterday, and push them far past tomorrow. I recalled my experiences with the poor I lived with on Crete and the needs of a nomadic people on the edges of Iraq and Turkey; and further took to heart the lessons of the misguided missionaries that pacified to their standards, the natives that were already living a happy life: I considered the consequences that ensued. It was then the 9 Tomatoes a Day program just popped into my head. It was complete. Every detail instantly revealed.

"The answer to all Haiti's problems laid in helping the poorest among them to reach some sort of economic and agricultural stability that helped to maintain some level of personal happiness. It was clear, only from the bottom up could the country be successfully rebuilt. Money paid to the top levels would never reach the needs of the bottom levels. Building stability and hope was more important than immediately building infrastructure. Again, trying anything from the top down would be a tried and proven catastrophe. If these considerations were the focus of the plan, the rest would evolve on its own.

"There was a large leap of faith that the 9 Tomato program combined with anaerobic digesters would make so much sense that the message of why it was needed would carry the entire effort forward. Time will tell if I was right."

Stone had developed a deep respect and appreciation for Sean. He was a no nonsense guy who also wanted to make a difference, and he did not suffer fools lightly.

Sean stood up, smiled, and shook Stone's hand before jumping onto the dock. Nothing needed saying. Their actions were enough.

Back home, Madame Louise-Perrier sat on the edge of her bed preparing for sleep. She looked over the pictures that adorned her nightstand while she brushed her hair. Looking back was her mother, her grandmother, and a sketch of her greatest blood ancestor, one of the Hispaniola slaves who help win the rebellion that ignited the spark leading to Hope. Adanech's story, of capture and survival, had passed from generation to generation along with her life's mission, survive so one day you can make a difference. Madame Louise-Perrier smiled her knowing smile and with misty eyes said, "You have thank-you."

27

Epilogue

In the end, all we can do is trim our sails and ride out the storms with the knowledge that when the sun comes out and we reach the edge, a rainbow awaits us.

Thirty years after that memorable night on the porch of the Officers Club with his base commander and the lessons revealed there, Stone realized that we are all sheep, wolves, and shepherds molded into one, and that all of us, no matter the mix, will have the same destination. What makes each of us different is what we decide to leave behind as our legacy.

Never before, in Earth's long history had there been an experiment as insignificant as humanities' that could nonetheless yield such a potentially magnificent result, if only they could agree upon a common purpose, a common legacy. Perhaps here they had.

Stone reflected on the fact that all of humanity is on a journey, and as Homer wrote, the journey is all that counts. In the end, the journey is all we really have. It is during our Odysseys that our individual natures and potentials unfold, and our stories are recorded. All stories peak in the moments when our journeys bring us to forks in the road that challenge us to decide who we will become next, and that is when our potential is tested. In the end, if we survive and endure the tests, bastards and angels will eventually collide and the confluence of stories will ascend while merging into a mosaic of humanity's truest and best nature for all to admire. It is then humanity will *earn* the right to know a god.

Until that time, even with a meaningless lifetime backed by accumulated wealth, every story ends with the same revelations. That is, no one leaves this world alive: There are no pockets in heaven or hell: But mostly, the only wealth you take with you is the memories of footprints left behind that define your individual story. In this case, a story that tells what you did to tone down the insanity that would otherwise be left in your wake.

On this day of revelations and common purpose, quality of life now becomes the new gold standard, superseding gross national product. In this moment of enlightened transformation, our humanity begins to yield a purpose greater than self-interest while our individual stories become even more interesting.

Jacques the con man became the Executive Business Manager for all the cooperatives in Haiti. His years on the street making deals to find food and talking his way out of beatings and arrests paved the way for Jacques to become one of the leading executives of Haiti. The owners of the cooperatives trusted their lives and work to his judgment, and he never let them down. He turned down a corporate jet that would speed his worldwide travel to meetings that required his attention. He chose instead to fly coach, remembering that he was spending the money of friends who were still working the fields. People do see him shining, not with diamonds and gold that he wished for in his youth, but now with his good works in helping others to find dignity.

Pierre the protector became the commandant of police. Pierre grew to become one of the most respected and trusted men in Haiti. He protected the people under his care as he did his friends and family. The only people who feared him were criminals. Buck was there to help with them. The limousine he drives is his police car. One he is allowed to use to take his beautiful wife and sons to the beach or dinner. His mansion is a 450 square foot dwelling filled with love from his family, the glory of his every day actions that protect his nation, and the undying respect of his community.

Michel, the leader by example, became the Farm Manager for all the cooperatives. Despite the toil and hardships of working the land, his inner poet began to expand growing tentacles that inspired all who met him. His admiration for the Earth and its nature pours out of him in every class of farmers he teaches, and every excursion he takes to the groves to visit and talk with his trees. Michel became the inspiration and the glue that has held the farmers together in good and bad times. His loving mother continues to make gravy for his Sunday dinner: a humble reminder that it is the simple things in life, which bring the best flavors to one's primal hungers.

The "9 Tomatoes Celebrity Challenge" started gearing up for two more farms and seasons. Multi-national corporations got on the bandwagon and geared their marketing towards purpose advertising, showing how their products could aid humanity in real time.

The 9 Tomatoes Celebrity Challenge was a huge success. Over 30 million viewers located in England, France, Canada and America watched and supported their favorite coaches by texting in donations that averaged $25 USD each, enough to build 5 more farms.

Forrest brought back to America his new love for the earth and farming. He began building farming cooperatives nationwide in America to help bring opportunity and dignity to the poorest: all once living without work or home ownership. These farms began to turn the demand away from oil dependency, back towards farm-raised bio-fuels, which reduce America's green house gas emissions by over sixty percent.

Remy's Hard Rock Café is full every time a cruise ship stops in port. When the ships are not in port, the locals take up the extra space. The farm cooperatives are a must-visit when tourists stop by. As a result, the middle-income bracket of Haitian jobs in Ft. Liberte' started to swell the economy.

A number of the first celebrity participants built vacation homes in a little Tuscany styled village built on the mountainside overlooking a reservoir that supplies a hydropower plant: funded by the United Nations. David Fallon bought three condominium units that his family could use.

Sean Glenn went on to set up a program in Nigeria with the help of Shell Corporation, and the other movie stars moved on with their careers but always talked about the most important role they ever played in their lives while in Haiti.

Matt Ramon installs drinking water wells around the world and still helps to support and train the orphans of Haiti who live in the farming cooperatives.

It was a surprise when Michel Martelly, an entertainer better known as 'Sweet Micky' was elected president, winning 68% of the votes. He was able to break the political gridlock that threatened to plague his administration, by unveiling a plan to duplicate across the country farms like HOPE that promised new beginnings. He worked for the next few years to clean out corruption from government facilities and the Parliament. Those who were under suspicion knew he had a very persuasive friend nearby if things did not go his way.

Commandant Pierre became the new President's most trusted confidante. One day, at the President's request, Pierre drove him to a remote mountainside cabin. In it were many locked cells that contained the missing government officials and elite. Unlike the squalor the people under their fat thumbs once lived in, these corrupt leaders had clean water, sanitation, food, and a pillow. Among them was one very disgruntled ex-police commandant in a wheelchair. The President released a subtle smile and asked his security team to gather them up. They would stand trial in the new courthouse built from the earthquake rubble. A building that would forever mark this moment in time and be a reminder of Haiti's troubled past and how the people worked together building a bright future. Their trials would be presided over by persons who earned respect while defining leadership and good judgment through their actions during times of trouble, and a jury selected from the new voices of Haiti.

TJ changed his swing; completed designs for golf courses on two more farms, and won the next Masters Tournament he entered.

Ben Ackleff accepted the leading role for the upcoming movie based on the reality show and the convergence of lives that lead to its development.

If Stone had a fear, he only disclosed it to his closest friends. It was, in the moments before his death he would realize no one wanted to read his life story. It was as if he walked the earth as a ghost. He knew it was also a fear shared by many. That was until the stories of 200,000 people in Haiti ended in a horrific way but later manifested into a heroic accomplishment. Their deaths woke sleeping giants, otherwise ordinary people, who were also in pain and looking for a cure. The Haitian deaths brought dramatic improvements to the lives of many once living in poverty while also causing a global economic and humanitarian revival that cost just 9 Tomatoes a Day. Stone felt his fear subside when he imagined the power behind the blending of all the individual stories that merged into one heroic event that trumped over tragedy, greed, and corruption: Helping the poorest to ignite their lives by simply setting up opportunities. Now satisfied he had done his part to help ignite a passion for a common purpose humanity could enjoin, Stone sailed out of Liberte' Channel: he had no fondness for micro-details.

The Sun was beginning to set, and there was a gentle roll of waves in the following sea. Stone set the sails and made a cocktail. He lit a fresh Cuban cigar just before the arrival of his favorite moment while sailing. Just then, he leaned over and cut the engines. A quiet calm swam over the evening just as a fresh breeze filled the sails, causing the *Spiritus* to spring forward like a thoroughbred. The only sound heard came from the waves gently lapping against the hull and the whispered inspirations carried by the wind. Three small sea birds landed next to him, wanting only to share in the tranquil setting—perhaps messengers from some yet un-measured force.

Next Janet, his interpreter, who was so inspired as to enlist as the ship's first mate, climbed into the cockpit. She brightened the moment further with her naked presence. The feathered hitchhikers jumped on to her slender extended arm, seeming to care as little as she did about the destination, but wanting instead simply to enjoy the new, uncharted journey. She moved closer to Stone and while smiling asked,

"So you even charm little birds, what other tricks do I need to know about."

Stone thought to himself, she is really going to be trouble for someone. Stone set the autopilot to somewhere east and started to draw down his cigar. "The wind has brought us this far," he mused. "Let's see where it will take us next."

In the background Bob Marley began singing softly, "Don't worry about a thing…for every little thing gonna be alright"

THE END OF BOOK ONE

LET US BUILD FARM COOPERATIVES

Imagine the impact on our global economy creating 3 billion new consumers. Let us begin the conversation while building an army of doers all with the goal of making a better world. Imagine solving multiple problems at the same time with the same dollar!

Go to www.9tomatoesaday.com and tell us what you can do. Let us begin the task of moving one shovel of dirt first, followed by the next. If we wait for government to create change, the building wave of troubles will only continue to grow. Taking action now, is in our collective interest. Send no money! There is no formal organization. When it is decided, there is genuine interest; a full-born effort will ensue. In the mean time, traditional criteria establish if a large enough audience and backing awaits this epic effort. Here are the goals; you know the purpose:

1. Drive 15 million people to www.9tomatoesaday.com having them sign up indicating they would watch **the** 9 Tomato reality show build its first farm, prime time on a major network.

2. Fill in the blanks where you can, telling us what products you like. The reason should be obvious. Advertisers will be more interested in helping to air the show if they know their customers are cheering their good work. This information will help to pitch the purpose-oriented programming to the networks and to targeted advertisers.

3. One dollar from every paperback book sold will fund site planning, and the engineering and environmental surveys for the project should it proceed.

4. By 21 December 2012, instead of the world ending, humanity steps-up to change the world in which it lives!

LOVE TO HEAR YOUR THOUGHTS. **SIGN ON!** YOU KNOW WHO LOVES YA!

ONE BATTLE HAS BEEN WON IN HAITI, BUT THERE ARE MORE ON THE HORIZON AS STONE RICHARDS TRAVELS FROM ONE HOT SPOT TO ANOTHER.

Charles S. Darwin III

Once again, Stone Richards sails into a sea of trouble offering solutions that we can use in this reality.

Bunkering by crooks and terrorists has caused the entire Niger Delta to be flooded with oil, killing mangroves and seagrass that formed the basis of a food chain that once fed millions of people: Fishing communities, once thriving, are now starving and destitute; reasons for the youth to join with terror groups continue to grow. Shell Oil is losing millions of dollars in revenues every day as their employees are kidnapped, while trying to plug the vandalized pipelines. Stone sails into action and helps to frame a solution that turns crooks into heroes and helps to restore the livelihoods of thousands of villages that line the delta. COMING Spring 2012!

Read the second book in the Stone Richards Trilogy 'NIGER DELTA BLUES.' Learn about remarkable plans to rebuild the delta that help to restore the world's largest seafood nursery, and the global economy. Cringe from the clandestine battles required to make it happen. Fiction, once again, can become reality.

Watch for the 2012 release of the third book in the Stone Richards Trilogy— *The Dollars of Death*!

After building farm cooperatives in **9 TOMATOES A DAY** and cleaning up the worlds worse undisclosed oil spill in the **NIGER DELTA BLUES** and exposing a Middle Eastern counterfeiting ring that threatened to destroy the worlds economy in **Dollars of Death**, something more powerful is needed to set right the hideous wrongs committed by the worlds most powerful people. Now Stone Richards gains supernatural powers from a freak galactic event that allows him to effortlessly 'Phase Walk' through time and space. As always, after learning what his new abilities are, he goes about fulfilling his life's mission to help others in the first book of the next STONE RICHARDS SERIES--PHASED WALKING: I BEATI PAOLI and THE DEVILS HAND.

AVAILABLE NOW!

Stone Richards survives a horrific storm at sea ending up a cast away on a desolate volcanic island in the south pacific. There he endures a galactic ordeal that seemingly leaves him with supernatural powers, which allow him to change the world in ways no sane person could ever imagine. To Stone, however, nothing is supernatural everything can be explained. And that is what he does while 'Phase Walking' from one global destination to another, enlisting the resources of quantum powers to heal past environmental and economic wrongs establishing, once and for all time, a new sustainable path for humanity to travel.

The adventures have just begun, and challenges still await us.